THE CASE OF THE CHRISTMAS ORNAMENT KILLER:

A DETECTIVE TOM GRANT INVESTIGATION

RONALD A. ROWBOTTOM

The Case of the Christmas Ornament Killer:
A Detective Tom Grant Investigation

Copyright © 2022 by Ronald A. Rowbottom

Bennett books may be ordered through booksellers or by contacting:

Bennett Media and Marketing
1603 Capitol Ave., Suite 310 A233
Cheyenne, WY 82001
www.thebennettmediaandmarketing.com
Phone: 1-307-202-9292

Because of the dynamic nature of the Internet, any web addresses or links contained in this book may have changed since publication and may no longer be valid. The views expressed in this work are solely those of the author and do not necessarily reflect the views of the publisher, and the publisher hereby disclaims any responsibility for them.

Any people depicted in stock imagery provided by Shutterstock are models, and such images are being used for illustrative purposes only.

Certain stock imagery © Shutterstock

ISBN: 978-1-957114-36-1 (Paperback)
ISBN: 978-1-957114-37-8 (eBook)

Printed in the United States of America

As always, this novel is dedicated to my friend and companion of fifty-two years, Teddy Rowbottom. You have stood by me throughout all of our life's journey and been the anchor for our daughter and two sons. I also dedicate this to my two outstanding adult grandchildren, Kobe and Trinity.

In addition, I want to acknowledge and thank Scott Scherer of London Ontario for his assistance as a BETA Reader of my draft.

Chapter One

It was Friday evening December 3rd, 1993 when Nancy Graves left work at the office and headed over to her parents' home. She had just turned twenty-three years old today and was celebrating by having dinner at her parent's place and then meeting with friends from the office where she worked.,

At the home of her mother Helen and stepfather George Perkins she settled into the comfortable routine of talking with her younger sister Betty as Helen and George finished setting out the dinner on the dining room table.

The house was decorated for Christmas with decoration keepsakes that Nancy had seen every year of her life. Nancy felt comfortable and relaxed in the home that had provided a stable environment where she and Betty had been raised to adulthood. There had been times of trouble but Nancy was always able to come through the concerns.

Nancy graduated from the Paralegal Degree Program at Fanshawe College in London and got a job working as a licenced paralegal in a local law firm. She had moved out on her own this past summer. The independence felt good but there were times when she missed the comfort and stability of having her family around her every day.

Betty remarked that the same old decorations had been on their Christmas tree for all of the twenty-one years of her life and wondered why mom and dad never got rid of any of the old, tattered items.

"Its because they have meaning," Nancy commented, "They each represent memories of our lives together even before our father died."

Nancy had just turned thirteen when she watched her father suffer from a rapid form of brain cancer that took his life. George had come into their lives and married their mom two years after their dad had passed away and filled a big hole in their mom's life as well as their own.

She had become a troubled teenager and was headed down a dark path until George had married her mom and showed love for the girls as if they were his own daughters. He never tried to replace their father but he was always there for them and as a fifteen-year-old bitter youth Nancy had needed that support more then she realized at the time.

They had formed a new family.

Helen announced that supper was on the table and the family settled down to a meal sharing stories and memories about Nancy. Following supper George brought in a birthday cake from the kitchen covered with twenty-three burning candles that made Nancy remark that they should call the fire department. After three attempts all the candles were extinguished and everyone settled into eating their share of the cake.

"There is nearly half the cake left," Helen remarked, "Do you want to take it to your apartment and have it for leftovers?"

"Thanks Mom," Nancy replied, "but I am meeting a couple of girl friends from the office so I will just leave it here. If dad and Betty have left any I'll have another piece on Sunday when I come over,

George offered to give Nancy a ride to the wine bar. Nancy said her good-byes with hugs all around and they left just after eight p.m.

Nancy entered the wine bar and saw her friends in a corner table. The girls greeted each other and Bridgett ordered a glass of wine for Nancy and refills for each of them.

The atmosphere in the wine bar was subdued and Nancy liked it that way, no raucous partiers or drunken "studs" as they liked to call the guys that frequented the bars and spurted out the most ridiculous pick up lines.

Nancy did not have a steady boy friend at this point in her life and had come to the realization she preferred the company of other women. She had gone out on sporadic dates with men in college but never really felt they had clicked

The friends sat and chatted for the next few hours until eleven p.m. when they mutually agreed it was time to split up and head to their various homes.

Nancy's apartment was just ten blocks from the wine bar so she decided not to bother with a ride and to walk home. Louise and Bridgett had called a Taxi and were waiting outside at the curb as Nancy walked away.

Nancy was just a block away from her apartment building when she walked past an open alleyway. She felt someone grab her from behind grasping a cloth over her mouth and nose. She tried to struggle but quickly felt herself sinking into unconsciousness.

Nancy awoke in a dimly lit empty room except for an old chair in the corner. She felt groggy as she tried to lift her arms but they were unable to move. She slowly realized that her arms and legs were tied to four metal loops in the floor with cord that stretched her body spread eagle. The sensation of plastic on her bare back filled her with terror as she came to the realization that she was lying on a rubber sheet on the floor and that she was naked.

She tried to scream but nothing came out of her mouth through the duct tape that was bound across her mouth and lower face.

"There's no sense struggling to escape," a voice spoke slowly in the darkness of the room, "the cords are strong and the anchors in the floor are secured."

The voice was muffled and deep but Nancy knew it was a man's voice.

"Don't worry as we are going to have some fun." Remarked the bodyless voice.

Suddenly a man appeared in her vision and she could see that he was dressed in a rubber suit like swimmers wore for scuba diving.

The steel of a razor knife glinted in the half light and Nancy felt as though her heart leaped into her throat in terror.

Slowly the man started to cut lines into Nancy's flesh on her stomach as she flinched in pain, unable to stop what was happening to her body.

CHAPTER TWO

Detective Tom Grant had joined the police force in 1975 after he completed the Sociology Undergraduate program in Criminology at Western University in London. The outline description had caught his attention and intrigued him:

'Criminology is the study of the nature, extent, causes, and consequences of crime and criminal behaviour in society. The nature of the criminal justice system and the experiences of those involved in it – including offenders, victims, police officer and others.'

Tom had then taken the Police Officers Diploma Program offered at a local college before applying for the police force.

The next eighteen years of his career he worked as a constable in the Uniformed Division on the streets of London. He had been part of the Community Policing Section serving in the community foot patrol unit before moving through the community service unit, crime prevention, alternate response section, as well as the emergency response section.

Tom had been promoted to detective in the Major Crimes Unit of the London Police Force in April of the year 1993. And held a deep conviction that what he was doing was helping people as he strived for ways that he could live up to the motto of the force "Facta Non Verba" Latin for "Deeds Not Words".

Tom and his spouse Ann had met in 1971 in his hometown of Simcoe Ontario where both had grown up. Ann often shared the story of how she had seen him at the local skating rink roller skating and something had told her that 'he was the one for her' in her mind.

Ann was a clean cut eighteen-year-old and part of a family of church goers. Tom was an eighteen-year-old graduate of Simcoe Composite School who had the look of one who was into the mode of the seventies. He had long hair and mutton chop sideburns, wore head bands, granny glasses and purple bell bottom jeans. The old adage of opposites attracts seemed to be a fitting description.

Later that week Ann and Tom had been introduced at a party at a mutual friend's home and became a couple from that moment forward.

Tom was registered to go to Western University that fall to start his degree program and in August after they had known each other for just three months it seemed a natural thing for them to decided to get married.

Ann had her final year of high school to complete so the couple decided to wait till June of the next year to have the wedding.

Having made the decision there was just one thing left that Ann needed to do. Her parents had not met Tom at this point and she was concerned how they would react to their decision.

During the first week of October every year the Norfolk County Fair was held in Simcoe and Tom would be home for the Thanksgiving Weekend. They planned to go the fairgrounds that Saturday. Ann's parents were attending the Saturday evening grandstand show and Ann decided to take the opportunity to approach her parents and introduce Tom to them.

The next morning was Sunday and as the family prepared to attend church Ann talked with her parents in the kitchen and proceeded to tell them that her and Tom had agreed to be married the next June.

Her mother's reaction was, "Is this because you have to get married?'

"No, we love each other and want to get married and I am not pregnant."

Her father's reaction was more subdued and he sat down with Ann at the kitchen table and just talked about their decision and if Ann had truly thought through this and was sure.

Ann's dad was an elder in the Community of Christ church that they attended and he concluded by asking if Tom would come over that evening for supper so they could get to know him before they made any further statements.

Ann agreed to call Tom and ask him. She always loved how her father looked at things rationally and calmly which was the opposite of her mother. Her dad was the glue that held the family together.

Her younger brother who had been standing in the kitchen by the sink then broke the tension with the comment.

"When mom came home last night, she was talking about the young man you introduced them too with his long hair, beaded head band, purple bell bottom blue jeans and sandals. Little did she realize that you were setting them up for the kill. Well played sis."

Ann's mom simply glared at him and stated. "Its time we all left for church service and I would appreciate it if you kept your comments to yourself."

That evening Tom arrived at their home for supper and Ann had advised him to wear regular jeans and lose the head band which Tom had obliged. The conversation was somewhat stilted as the family got to know Tom, what his plans were for his life and his goals.

Things went relatively well as they discussed the June wedding. Tom told them he had grown up Anglican and lived in the house that was just two homes further up the street from the Community of Christs small white church.

His parents had met Ann that summer and were now aware of their decision to get married. It was agreed that Tom and Ann would get married in her church and Tom's parents had offered to hold the small reception in their home. Ann mentioned that she would like her uncle Jack to perform the ceremony so by the time dinner was over the tensions had eased.

Ann's mom only made one last statement while she was washing the dishes in the sink.

She looked at Ann and brought up the nice church boy who lived down the street. "I always wanted you to get to know him and go out with that boy but I guess that's not a possibility now."

Ann looked at Tom and grimaced saliently mouthing the word sorry.

Over the years since they had married Tom had become a favorite to Ann's mom and if anyone brought up the statement over the dishes that first night she would adamantly deny having said it and would respond with a wounded tone in her voice "Why would you make up a story and say such a thing about me."

Ann and Tom had married June 3rd, 1972 at the little white Community of Christ church Anns family attended on the street he had grown up on. The small gathering of some thirty family and friends met at the church at 10:00 a.m. on that Saturday morning to be part of their marriage officiated by Ann's uncle.

Ann's family were opposed to drinking alcohol but Tom's family was not. His dad had emigrated from Wales to Canada in his early years and drinking was a part of how you celebrated. To accommodate Ann's family Toms dad had put the alcohol in his brothers' home which was just a block away. His side of the family would slip out sporadically and go over to his brother's place.

Tom's dad at one point asked Ann's dad if he would like to come over to his brother's house with him. Ann's mom heard it and responded, "No he would not."

Ann and Tom smiled at each other and Ann remembered that as a child growing up her father had been a firefighter in Simcoe during her early years. She remembered that they lived in an apartment above the firehall and her dad would go down at night into the firehall meeting room and talk with the other fire fighters. He was not opposed to having a drink back then but one night her mother sent Ann down to get her dad for supper.

He was sitting at the table talking and had an open beer bottle on the table. Ann had been a curious child and she asked her dad if she could taste it. He said okay and Ann had picked up the bottle and drank down a huge gulp of beer before her dad could stop her. As an eight-year-old who had never tasted alcohol before she immediately became sick to her stomach.

When her mother found out what had happened it turned into a bad night for her dad as she tore a verbal strip off her father.

Ann could never stand beer after that and even the smell made her feel nauseated. As for her father she never saw him drink again and her mother would make sure to proclaim that her dad was a non-drinker when it came to alcohol.

That summer Tom and Ann had become a part of a group of friends who had started a drop-in center and helpline in Simcoe called Project Hope.

One of the main crops grown in the area was Tobacco which was labour intensive and attracted transient workers from across the provinces to work in the harvest. Tom had worked in the tobacco fields since he was a youth and at the age of fifteen had become a "primer" who harvested the tobacco leaves in the fields. It was decent money and as a summer job provided a good summer income.

That July when the tobacco transient workers from Quebec and other places arrived in Simcoe to work the tobacco harvest there was an issue. The late spring had delayed the tobacco crop and the workers had arrived two weeks early. They had no places to stay or eat since the Salvation Army generally ran the soup kitchens and provided food until the harvest started. The Salvation Army was not going to open for meals for that two-week period.

Tom on behalf of Project Help had approach the Pastor and Elders of the Community of Christ church in Simcoe where they had been married. The small white church building had a small kitchen and fellowship hall downstairs that would sit around 50 people.

The neighbourhood was a quiet residential street.

When Tom approached the elders and asked if they could use the basement fellowship hall to feed between 300 and 400 people a day for two meals, he was not sure how they would react.

The Pastor and Elders which included Ann's father had not hesitated and agreed to trust Tom and the volunteers, so Project Help ran a soup kitchen for 10 days that summer from the basement of that little white church until the Salvation Soup Kitchen opened.

Tom often accredited his conversion to his wife's denomination as the result of the willingness and compassion of the members of the little church that summer and had been a member ever since.

Tom and Ann had moved to London that fall and started their lives together as a married couple. Their family grew when their oldest son, Tom jr was born in 1986.

Tom was promoted to the major crime division in April 1993 and with their second child due to arrive in the fall they had decided it was time to buy a home of their own after living for eighteen years in rental condo's around London.

Ann and Tom looked at new houses being built in the northern part of the city and decided on a four-bedroom residence located in a family-oriented neighbourhood. There were highly rated schools in the area and it just felt like home from the moment they had walked in with the realtor that represented the builder. The house was finished on the exterior and they still had the opportunity to decide the finishes for the interior for completion before their scheduled possession date of August 1993.

Everything went smoothly and the family moved into their new home September the 1st followed in mid October with the arrival of an eight-pound four-ounce baby boy they named Kevin.

New position at work, expanding family, and a home of their own. It seemed to Tom that everything was progressing as it should in their lives.

Tom was assigned as a junior detective working under the mentorship of veteran Detective Ed Morgan. Ed was a legend in the department having worked a total of forty-four years in the London police force with an impressive rate for solving cases.

Tom had learned over the eight months that he had been working under Ed's leadership that he was an abrupt teacher and could be extremely brisk in his interactions with Tom He would not hesitate to criticize Tom but Tom realized that the intentions were to make him a better detective and deep-down Tom appreciated it. Although there were times when Tom would have relished replying to Ed's cranky nature with comments of his own.

CHAPTER THREE

Monday morning December 6th, 1993, Tom arrived at the station at 7:45 and proceeded to his desk in the communal office space shared by the junior detectives referred to as the Detectives bull pen. He had a desk, chair and a small two drawer filing cabinet within his designated workspace. The filing cabinet was for current ongoing cases and once a case was resolved the files would be routinely purged into the main file storage room as a more permanent home.

Tom was equipped with a cell phone, desk phone and desk top computer. Drinking coffee was not allowed at the workstations for the junior detectives even though the senior detectives could drink coffee in their private offices.

He appreciated the times during the day when Ed would yell for him to come to his office and Tom could arrive with two cups of coffee. One for himself and one for Ed.

Tom and Ann had spent the last two weekends in their new home adjusting to life again with a new baby and putting up the Christmas decorations both inside the home and outside.

It was a new experience for Tom to be on a ladder stringing exterior lights around the eve troughs and the peak of the home which had left him wondering if this was the smart thing or if he should pay someone.

Doing the interior was another matter as Tom loved putting up the Christmas Tree, hanging the stockings on the mantel of the fireplace and setting out everything else. Ann and Tom had received a ceramic Christmas Tree as a wedding present and they carefully packed it away every year and brought it out again every Christmas along with a Nativity scene that Ann had owned since she was a child. Seven-year-old Tom Jr was continuously under foot with excitement as they decorated their home trying to "help" unpack the ornaments and yelling at his baby brother to look and see. Kevin simply laid oblivious of everything in his crib which made Tom Jr try all the harder.

At 8:15 Tom heard the voice of Ed Morgan bellowing from his office for Tom to get in there. Grabbing his usual supply of coffee's Tom went into Ed's office.

Ed was in his sixties but no one was really sure of his age nor would they guess when he was within ear shot. He was considered well built which other detectives referred to as overweight but never in the presence of the great Ed Morgan. His suit always looked like it needed a fresh press with his top shirt button undone and his tie hanging loosely around his neck.

Tom on the other hand was always neatly dressed in his black suit and tie, his short cut brown hair was neat in what Tom considered presentable for a detective in the force. He prided himself in his appearance and the shape that he was in for a forty-one-year-old.

"Tom, I need your help on this dam computer," Ed barked.

Ed was a great detective but had not adjusted well to the electronic policing age and still preferred phone calls and writing pads.

Tom gave Ed his coffee and proceeded over to the computer screen. The screen was displaying a message stating that Ed had mail which obviously meant nothing to Ed. Tom went into Ed's email account and pulled up a new email that was sitting in the in box.

"There," Tom replied, "your mailbox is open and you can read the email."

"Don't be daft," Ed stated, "just read the dam thing out loud."

Tom opened the email and proceeded to read the message.

"You don't know me but I know you." It started, "I have left a Christmas present for you and your detective friends in the upstairs room of the old abandoned warehouse at 1700 Clarke road in the east end. Marry Xmas." Signed Santa Clause.

Ed and Tom looked at each other and Tom tried to get an email address where the email had come from but it had no computer address.

"I can get the cyber team to try and locate the location where it was logged on and sent from?" Tom commented.

"What for? Its probably some nut case looking for attention. I'll ask for a uniform officer to go to the address he listed just to be thorough." Ed remarked.

Tom contacted the uniformed officer department and asked the duty officer to have a patrol check out the building. He also forwarded the email to the cyber team to see if they could identify where the email had originated.

They then proceeded to spend time looking over the open cases that they were currently working on and preparing for an upcoming trial that was scheduled for two individuals who had been caught breaking and entering stores in downtown London.

It was just over an hour later when Ed's phone rang. It was the uniformed officer lead calling to advise Ed that the uniformed officers had located a body in the upstairs room of the building who's address Tom had provided.

The Crime Identification Department (CID) team had been dispatched along with the coroner. "It's a pretty ugly scene" he commented "and you will need a strong stomach based on what the uniformed officers have told me."

Ed and Tom grabbed their coats and left the station proceeding in Ed's car to the crime scene.

The warehouse was cordoned off with police caution tape and the CID van was on the scene. In addition, Tom noted that the coroners van was also parked out front. The flashing lights and activity had attracted a good size crowd of Onlookers including the ever-present members of the press who seemed to be the first to arrive after a crime scene or accident had been identified.

They proceeded to enter the building and climbed the stairs to the second-floor location of the crime. When Tom Ornented, he was shocked by the scene before him. A young lady in her mid twenties was tied naked and spread eagle on her back on the floor. Her hands and feet had been staked out by tying cords to metal hooks that were screwed into the wooden floor. Over her head hung a plastic clump of mistletoe and into the flesh of her abdomen was cut the words Merry Xmas. Her mouth was loosely covered by duct tape and a plastic bag had been placed over her head and duct tapped at the throat.

On her arms and legs and other parts of her body were deep angry wounds that sliced into her body.

"It appears she likely died from suffocation due to the plastic bag" the coroner commented "but we will need to get her to the autopsy room to be sure.

Based on the amount of bleeding and appearance of the wounds that were inflicted they were done prior to death so she was likely alive during the incisions.

We need to look in her mouth as there is an object showing there once the CID have finished so we can remove the plastic bag."

Tom and Ed waited as the forensics team did their work.

Tom had seen terrible sights during his years on the uniformed officers team visiting horrific accident scenes and tragic domestic violence cases but none of those could prepare him for what he was looking at now.

The CID team lead advised them that they had located a pile of women's clothes in the corner of the room on the chair and he brought over the small black clutch handbag that was lying on top of the pile. They had dusted the bag for prints and Ed was free to look inside for identification.

Inside they found the licence for Nancy Graves, age twenty-three as of last Friday and her address. Written on an emergency contact card were the names of Helen and George Perkins and their address. The women, Helen was identified as her mother on the card.

CID had finished processing the body and had moved to processing the balance of the room so the coroner proceeded to remove the plastic bag off the face of Nancy Graves. Stuck into her mouth the coroner found a small plastic Christmas Tree ornament. This was one of the cheap little white plastic Christmas tree bulbs of the type that could be found in any dollar store.

Based on the fact that it had not been broken the coroner advised that the ornament was likely put into the victim's mouth after she had suffocated and the perpetrator had re sealed the bag which explained why the plastic was loose and not sucked into the mouth as the victim chocked for air.

He estimated the time of death had occurred sometime Friday overnight based on the condition of the body and the fact that rigor mortis had fully dissipated. Lividity confirmed that the body had not been moved and was still in the same position it was at the time of death.

The coroner signaled the ambulance attendants to come in and remove the body on a covered stretcher so that the CID team could process the plastic sheet.

"It appears that the corkscrew hooks were simply screwed into the wooden floor using a wrench" the CID lead explained to the detectives. "We have processed the room for fingerprints and evidence and will take everything back to the lab for analysis. I'll email you a report of our findings etc. as soon as we can complete the work."

"Can you simply send me over a paper copy," Ed commented, "I am not keen on this electronic crap and want something I can review and sink my teeth into. You can send an electronic copy to Tom Grant here and the whiz kid can do what he wants with that."

"No problem" the lead remarked and smirked at Tom as he headed out the door to work with his team on processing the stairwell and the front entrance.

Tom and Ed headed down the stairs to the front door of the building knowing that the reality of the next couple of hours would be difficult as they went to visit Helen and George Perkins and inform them of the death of one Nancy Graves.

Ed called in to the deputy chief of Detectives and brought him up to date on the murder scene and advised him where they were heading. He told the deputy chief that they had been confronted by the press and advised them they had no comment at this time and that a statement would be made at some point by the London Police media officer who was currently at the scene.

Tom was quiet as they drove over to the address listed for Helen and George.

"First time you have seen something like that I assume," Ed asked.

Tom nodded in agreement.

"Well trust me, it does not get any easier but you will get use to observing the horrors in this job that people can do to one another. Our job is to find the sick scum that did this and make sure they spend the rest of their miserable lives not hurting anyone else.

Tom understood the rationale but the reality at this point was hard to process.

CHAPTER FOUR

When they arrived at the home of Helen and George, they were met at the door by a younger version of the victim they had just seen. She introduced herself as Betty Graves after which Tom and Ed introduced themselves and showed her their identification.

"Are Helen and George Perkins at home? "they asked.

"They should be back momentarily. My sister did not show up for dinner yesterday and has not come into work this morning so they went over to her apartment to check on her. Can I ask what this is about?" she queried. Tom could sense the unease that was evident in her voice and on her face. "Has my sister been in an accident or something?"

"We will need to wait to talk to your parents before we can answer that question." Ed replied, "Can we come in?"

Betty led them into the living room and sat nervously on the chair staring at the floor.

Shortly they heard a car drive up into the driveway and a couple entered the home freezing in shock at the sight of the detectives sitting in the living room.

"Mom these are detectives from the police." Betty blurted.

Tom and Ed re introduced themselves and showed their credentials.

"Can we ask what your relationship is with Nancy graves." Ed queried.

"I am her mother and George is her stepfather. Her biological father died several years ago. We have not been able to contact Nancy is she hurt or injured." Helen responded.

"Mr. and Mrs. Perkins, we regret to inform you that your daughter was found murdered this morning in an abandoned warehouse on the east side."

Helen Perkins broke down in a wave of tears supported by her husband to keep her from falling to the floor. Tom looked at Betty and was torn by the look of utter despair that he saw.

George helped Helen to the coach and asked, "How can this be, what happened."

"We are in the early stages of our investigation and need to ask you some questions if you are able."

"Where is my daughter," Helen sobbed "I want to see my little girl."

"When did you all last see Nancy." Tom asked quietly.

"Friday evening, " George responded. "Nancy came over for her birthday dinner and I dropped her off at the wine bar on Richmond street. She was meeting a couple of her girl friends from work for a celebration drink."

"Where was Nancy employed?"

"My sister is a paralegal at the law offices of Miller and Shepherd." Betty stated.

Tom could see that Betty had still not comprehended the fact of her sister's death and was speaking in the present sense.

"Do you know the names of the friends she was meeting?" Ed asked.

"NO, just that they were friends from the office."

"MY daughter is a good girl and doesn't go out partying or anything like that. Why would anyone harm her?" Helen sobbed. "I want to see my daughter."

Ed advised the family that a patrol car was outside and that the officer would be available to drive them to the coroner's morgue located at University hospital in order to positively identify their daughter.

Tom and Ed escorted the family out to the patrol car and watched as they drove away with the uniformed officer. Ed called the coroner to advise him that the parents and sister of the victim were on their way to the morgue to identify their daughter.

"Thanks for the heads up, I have just finished cleaning up the body and haven't started the autopsy yet so I will wait till the family has left." The coroner proceeded to prepare the body on a stretcher covered with a sheet so that the family would only see the head and face of the victim.

This was the worst part of his job, having to see the faces and experience the emotion of the family members as the reality of their dead loved one is confronted.

Tom and Ed proceeded to the law offices of Miller and Shepherd.

The offices comprised the first floor of a small brick office building located on Wellington street north of the downtown.

They were greeted upon entry by a receptionist who was seated behind a glass partition that separated the main office from the front reception area.

"May I help you.? She asked.

Tom and Ed introduced themselves and showed their credentials before asking if they could speak with the two paralegals from this office who had been with Nancy Graves Friday evening at the wine bar.

"Nancy has not come into work today. We have been a little worried but we assume that she has taken a long weekend for her birthday and forgot to call."

"Can you please see if you can identify the two paralegals that were with her Friday evening so we can speak with them.? The receptionist's facial expression changed to one of concern. "Let me call Mr. Miller and he should be able to assist you." She replied.

Shortly thereafter a gentleman in his mid forties came out of the office area into the reception room and introduced himself as Paul Miller, a partner in the law firm.

He invited the detectives into a small conference room and then proceeded to ask what the reason for their visit was.

Ed explained that they were trying to track the actions of one Nancy Graves last Friday evening and they understood that she had met with two of the paralegals from the office.

"Nancy works here but she has not been into work today. Has something happened to Nancy?"

"We are not at liberty to discuss details but Ms. Graves was found deceased this morning."

"O my goodness." Paul stated. "Let me check with the paralegals and see if I can find out who was with her Friday evening."

Paul Miller left the conference room and returned shortly with two young ladies.

He introduced them as Louise Simpson and Bridgett Johnson and advised the detectives that they had been the two friends with Nancy on Friday night.

Tom and Ed re introduced themselves and showed their credentials.

"Is it true what Mr. Miller said, that Nancy is dead?" Asked Louise.

"We really need to find out from the two of you what transpired Friday evening." Tom asked.

"We went to wine bar to meet Nancy for a celebration drink. We planned to meet at 8:30 and Nancy arrived just around that time. We had a couple of glasses of wine and chatted until about 10:30 or so when we all left together. Nancy lives a few blocks from the wine bar and decided to walk home to her apartment while Bridgett and I called a taxi to pick us up and take us to our homes."

"How much did you all have to drink over the evening."

"Only three glasses of wine each. None of us were drunk or incapacitated in any way."

"Did you notice anyone hanging around your table or acting suspiciously during the evening?"

"Not that I can remember." Bridget commented,

"Same for me" replied Louise. "It was just a fun drink in a quiet wine bar, nothing suspicious. What happened to Nancy?"

"We can not comment on an ongoing investigation at this time but we appreciate your help. Nancy didn't indicate that she would be meeting anyone else later that evening?"

"No, she said she was walking straight home because she was a little tired."

"Thanks for your assistance, we appreciate your willingness to help." Ed commented and then they left the law office.

Next on the list was to visit Nancy Graves apartment located on Richmond street in downtown London. It was only a five-minute drive or a fifteen-minute walk from the law office.

They drove past the wine bar in question on route to her apartment and noted the need to stop in later today after the bar opened to talk with the staff.

Nancy's small one-bedroom apartment was on the fifth floor of the apartment building. The building superintendent provided access to the apartment when they advised that they were looking into the suspicious death of Nancy Graves, the tenant.

In searching through the room, they found no indication that anyone else whether male or female had been present in the apartment due to no extra clothes, toothbrushes, etc. There were several framed photos of her parents and her sister throughout the apartment. In addition, there was one unframed photo of herself with a young man which appeared to be taken at the beach during the summer leaned up against the books on her bookshelf in the living room.

Ed took the photo from the bookshelf in order to question the Perkins regarding the identity of the young man.

Other then that the apartment was neat and tidy and had every indication that Nancy lived alone.

Tom questioned the superintendent and asked if he ever noticed others coming into or going from the building with Nancy graves.

"No, she was the quiet type, no party's, loud music, or issues with other tenants. She was friendly enough but the only visitors he had seen coming or going to the apartment were her parents and her younger sister."

Ed showed him the picture of Nancy and the young man and asked if he had ever seen this gentleman at the apartment and knew his name.

"Don't recognize him and can't say that I ever saw or met him."

"What happens now with the apartment?" the superintendent asked.

"Nancy's parents should be in touch regarding her things and the release of the apartment shortly when they have had time to adjust to their loss. In the meantime, this is still a private residence and no one goes in or nothing gets removed without discussing first with her parents."

The superintendent replied that he understood and locked the door to the apartment.

The detectives had worked past the normal lunch time so they headed back to the station. Tom had learned quickly that when it came to eating lunch Ed was old school. He brought his lunch everyday in a brown paper bag and ate at his desk, no going to restaurants for Ed.

He had advised Tom the first day that his lunch time was his alone down time and intended to keep it that way. Tom left the station and went down the street to a little deli that was within walking distance and ordered a sandwich. There were usually other detectives from the station at the same place but not today. It was past the regular lunch time crowd and Tom had the place basically to himself.

He sat at one of the small tables and reflected over everything from this morning. He found it hard to eat his sandwich as he pictured the crime scene in his mind and eventually gave up trying. He packed the sandwich remains in a to go box and headed back to the station.

In his mind he came to the realization that these may be the type of scenes he would be working for the balance of his career in the Major Crimes detective's unit and he would need to harden himself so that he could stay objective and do his job. He was sure that the scene was not interfering with Eds ability to eat his lunch.

He went to his desk and proceeded to put his notes from this morning into a more legible and organized format until he heard Ed bark loudly for him to come to his office..

He took the opportunity to grab two coffees on his way hoping that he would have time to drink his before they rolled out of the office.

Ed took his coffee and they sat and chatted over the mugs about the crime scene as Ed queried Tom about what he saw and what those things meant when assessing a scene.

About 3 p.m. Ed stated they had two actions left for the afternoon, one was to visit the home of the victim and see if the family could identify the young man in the photo and secondly to stop into the wine bar and question the staff about what they may have seen Friday evening.

When they arrived at the home of Nancy Graves family, they found that Helen and George were out making arrangements for their daughters' funeral but Betty was home.

Tom could see how distraught Betty was as she kept wiping her eyes with a Kleenex.

"Let me say again how sorry we are for your loss Ms. Graves but we just have a couple of questions we need to ask." Ed stated.

"My name is actually Betty Perkins, I took my stepfathers name. Do you have you any idea who did this to my sister?'

"We are still early in the investigation but I am confident we will identify the individual that murdered your sister. Can you tell me, did Nancy have any close friends or a boyfriend that she was involved with?"

"Nancy had lots of friends but most were girls that she knew from growing up and college. I wouldn't call them close friends more like acquaintances that you make as you grow up. She has never really had a steady boyfriend as she would have told me. We shared everything about our lives since we became close after our Father passed away."

Ed showed Betty the photo, "Can you identify the young man in this photo?"

"Sure, that's Brad Jones. Brad has a been a friend from childhood. He used to live on this street with his family and he went to the same college as Nancy. They liked to hang out together but they have never been an involved romantically. Nancy used to refer to Brad as her brother from another mother because they were comfortable just hanging out and talking together.

"Can you provide us his address and contact information?"

Betty went to the other room and came back with Brad Jones address and phone number on a piece of paper.

"I just realized I don't think anyone will have let Brad know what happened so he will probably not be aware that Nancy is gone." Betty remarked, "Can I have the picture of Nancy and Brad?"

"You have my word that once we are done with the investigation the picture will be returned to your family." And on that note Ed concluded the interview and they left the home of Helen and George Perkins.

As they drove over to the wine bar Ed had Tom call Brad Jones telephone number and see if they could arrange a meeting.

A young man answered the phone and Tom identified himself as a London police detective and requested if Brad could be available to come into the station to provide information regarding an ongoing investigation.

Brad asked what this was about and Tom advised him it would be best to discuss in person and that he was not involved as a suspect or anything in that regard, they just needed to talk with him for information he may be aware of regarding the investigation.

Brad agreed and said he worked the afternoon shift as a chef at a restaurant in downtown London but could come into the station in the morning at 10:00 a.m.

"That would be fine," Tom replied, "just ask the front desk for Tom Grant and Ed Morgan when you arrive."

"We appreciate your willingness to assist us in this regard and we will see you in the morning." Tom stated and finished the call.

Ed had arrived at the wine bar and found a parking space in the bar's patrons parking. They proceed into the establishment.

The bar was quiet. There was only a couple of gentlemen in suits in the establishment sipping red wine in a corner table with open portfolios spread out. They were obviously businessmen talking a deal away from their offices in a more private setting.

Tom mused to himself wondering what these two were so intently working on over a glass of wine that required anonymity.

Ed identified himself to the bartender and asked if he had been working the bar on the Friday evening of last week.

The bartender confirmed he had been working so Ed showed him the picture of Nancy Graves with Brad Jones, "We are interested in whether you noticed this young lady here in the bar Friday night between 8:30 and 10:30."

"Sure" he replied, "Have never seen the guy before but she was here with two other ladies. They were having a couple of glasses of wine and talking. Nothing raucous just some laughing every once in a while, and it was the laughing that drew my attention. They seemed to be enjoying their evening."

"Did you notice them talk to anyone else during the time they were here or anyone hanging around near them?"

"Nope, we don't get any rough crowds in here so our patrons are pretty much a stay to themselves crowd, not the typical singles bar with pick up guys and girls looking for a good time if you know what I mean."

"How did the ladies look when they left?"

"Not drunk if that's what you mean, they each only had two or three glasses of wine during the time they were here."

'Did you notice if anyone followed them out as they left?"

"Not that I saw, mind if I might ask what is this all about?"

"One last question, have you noticed the lady in the picture in here before?"

"Occasionally I have seen her stop in a for a quick glass of wine which she mentioned she liked to do on her way home from work to unwind. Never more then one. She was always pleasant and friendly. What I would refer to as a classy lady."

"Thanks for your assistance we appreciate your help as we are trying to follow the steps this lady took Friday night, other then that we are not able to share any further details."

The detectives drove back to the station and Tom proceeded to pack up his desk in the bull pen and head home for the night.

As Tom arrived at home his legs were tackled by his seven-year-old son who wanted to let his dad know that his baby brother had laughed at him today after Tom Jr had come home from school. Tom sat down with his son and he told him that his little brother would need Tom Jr to make sure he set a good example since Kevin would be looking up to him. That was the role of big brothers.

Tom Jr was filled with pride that showed on his face as he proclaimed that he would be the best big brother ever.

Tom watched the six o'clock news as Ann finished supper and the first story was a report on the homicide that had happened in London's east end. The department media representative had held a press conference and advised that the body of a young woman had been found in an abandoned warehouse in London. Foul play was suspected but the investigation was in its early stages and more information would be available after the autopsy was complete.

"Was this drug or gang related?" questioned one of the reporters.

"We will not make any speculations at this point and the young ladies name is not being released at this time."

Tom watched as the camera showed the ambulance attendants exiting the warehouse with the body of Nancy Graves covered in a white sheet and invisible to the eyes of the by standers and press. Ann had entered the living room during the news cast and she asked if Tom was involved in the death that had been reported on the news.

He answered her that he was one of the two detectives that were investigating the case but could not provide any details. He did not tell Ann that the details were too horrifying to discuss with his family. It was obvious that Ann had grasped his reluctance and at that point they had reached an unspoken agreement regarding details about his work that would be their routine for the rest of their lives.

Tom had decided he would not discuss details of cases at work with his family, he needed to separate those two aspects of his life both for his own peace of mind and his families.

CHAPTER FIVE

At 10:00 a.m. the next morning Ed and Tom met with Brad Jones in the station conference room.

Brad was a young man that looked to be the same relative age as Nancy Graves.

When Ed asked him if he knew Nancy Graves and what their relationship was Brad told the detectives that Nancy and he had been friends since they were kids, growing up and playing together. They had both attended the same college in London where she took the paralegal course and he took the chef diploma program.

Brad asked what this was all about and Ed informed him that Nancy graves had been found deceased yesterday morning.

"We are trying to retrace her steps for last Friday evening and talking to friends who had known her."

"O my God," Brad interjected, "I was supposed to meet up with Nancy Saturday morning to go to the movies before my shift Saturday evening at the restaurant but she never showed up. I assumed she must have got tied up with family celebrating her birthday. I called and left a message on her cell phone voice mail but she never called back."

Tom made a note regarding Nancy's cell phone since that had not been found in her apartment or at the crime scene.

"Did you see Nancy Friday evening?"

"No, I work the evening shifts in the kitchen at the restaurant but I know she was going out with a couple of friends from work for a drink."

"We were wondering if you could elaborate on any boy friends or others that she had been involved with?"

"Nancy was never what you could call involved with anyone during her teen years or at college. She did go out occasionally but it was only for one or two dates and never developed into a serious relationship with anyone past that point.

"What about other friends she hung around with beside yourself?"

"Nancy talked about casual friends she had who worked with her and others she still talked to from our college days. Of course, her sister Betty and Nancy are very close."

"Is there anything else that you can think of that may be of help to us in our investigation?"

"Nothing that I can recall, how did Nancy die. Was it a car accident or something medical?"

"I am afraid we can not elaborate at this time as this is an on-going investigation, but we do appreciate your help."

Brad excused himself and left the station.

"It will be quite a shock for that young man when Nancy's name is released to the press and is identified as the body that was found in the abandoned warehouse. In addition, the public media team will be releasing some of the specifics of the homicide." Tom commented.

CHAPTER SIX

It was early the next week when Tom received an email from the coroner's office and from the CID team lead with the results of the autopsy and crime scene report.

Tom entered Ed's office and advised him he had received them on his computer which prompted Ed to exclaim. "I told them to send me the paper reports, have they not done that?"

"They are probably in the interoffice mail but I can print off the electronic reports and give you a paper copy."

"You should have done that already rather then coming in here and telling me you had them out there in cyber space." He barked.

Tom felt a twinge of anger but he quickly realized that Ed was Ed and he really did not mean anything by his remarks.

"I'll be back shortly with the reports."

"And don't forget my coffee when you come back." Ed mumbled.

Tom went back to his computer and proceeded to print off the coroner's autopsy and medical examiners report as well as the crime scene report.

He decided to skim through the documents before he headed back to Ed's office just so he would be prepared for any remarks, questions and comments.

The medical examiner / coroners report started with the standard answer to the five questions that were requirements as part of every report outlining the WHO (identity of the deceased),WHEN (date of death), WHERE (location of death), HOW (medical cause of death, and BY WHAT MEANS (natural causes, accident, homicide, suicide or undetermined).

The deceased is identified as *Nancy Graves age (23) twenty-three.*

Date of death: *December (3) third, (1993) nineteen ninety-three.*

Location of death: *an abandoned warehouse second floor, on Clarke Road, London, Ontario,*

Medical cause of death: *It was determined that the deceased died from asphyxiation caused by a plastic bag being sealed over her face,*

By what Means *Homicide.*

The medical examiners detail portion of the report outlined the condition of the body and any forensics obtained from the examination of the body.

'The deceased had evidence of duct tape over her mouth and on her throat that would have sealed the plastic bag over her head. The bag was inflated indicating that the plastic bag had been removed after the suffocation and then loosely reapplied over her head.

Located in the victim's mouth was a small plastic Christmas Ornament consisting of a tear drop shaped ball that was approximately two (2) inches in length and one (1) inch across. The object was white with a green snowflake design embossed on the sides and the words "Lets get Merry" on the snowflake.

A Photograph was taken of the object before Criminal Investigation Department officers took it into evidence for analysis.

Victim was naked and lying face up on a plastic sheet similar to those used as painters drop cloths. Her wrists and ankles were bound and tied by cords to metal hooks that were screwed into the floor creating circular bruising. This indicated that the victim would have been immobilized during the attack. There were a series of deep cut wounds in her arms, legs and breast area of the body that have the appearance of a razor knife or scalpel due to the size and shape of the incisions.

On the victims stomach the same instrument had been used to carve the words "Merry Xmas' into her flesh.

The appearance of the wounds and the blood flow at the scene indicates that the wounds had been made prior to death concluding that the victim was alive during the infliction of the incisions.

A small amount of a rubber like material was found in one of the incisions and has been sent to CID for analysis.

There were no apparent defensive wounds found on the victim.

A rape kit was undertaken, but there was no evidence of sexual activity and the rape kit came back negative.

Tom turned to the CID crime scene and analytical report:

The report first outlined the crime scene and included the photographs taken at the time of processing.

The room was approximately four and one half (4.5) meters by seven point six (7.6) meters.

The victim was lying in the center of the room on the wooden plank floor on top of a plastic drop cloth.

She was naked and bound in a spread-eagle position using cords that were tied on her wrists and ankles and secured by four twenty-one (21) centimeter hooks that were secured into the wood planking floor.

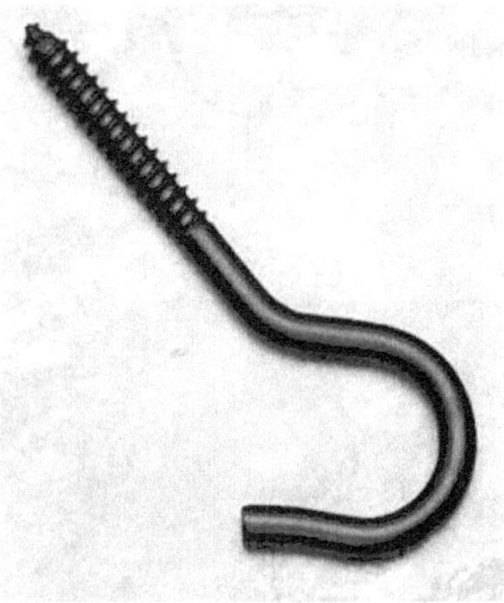

The hooks exhibited "teeth" marks from the tool, presumably a wrench, that was used to screw them into the wood plank flooring.

In the far corner of the room was a wooden chair that held the victims folded clothing. The clothes were analyzed and no fingerprints or other foreign matter was detected.

On top of the clothes was a small white cloth, analysis identified that the cloth contains remnants of an Ether like substance that is presumed to have been used to render the victim unconscious at some point during the abduction.

There was no electrical service turned on to the abandoned warehouse so it is assumed the perpetrator used some form of flashlight or lantern but there was nothing at the scene to verify or identify the device(s) used.

The drop cloth was a standard plastic cloth that can be purchased at local hardware or department stores and had no significant distinguishing characteristics.

Hung on the roof beam suspended above the victims face a string of plastic Mistletoe which was retrieved by CID. It had been hung from a nail with a burlap type string and both are available at numerous craft and hobby supply stores in the area.

The Plastic bag that had been taped over the victim's face was analysed and it contained the victims saliva but no other trace evidence on the interior or exterior of the bag or the tape that had been used to secure the bag across the victims mouth.

An object was retrieved from the victim's mouth consisting of a small Christmas tree type ornament referred to as a tear drop.

The object is approximately two (2) inches in length and one (1) inch across. It is white plastic with a green snowflake design embossed on the sides with the words "Lets get Merry" on the snowflake.

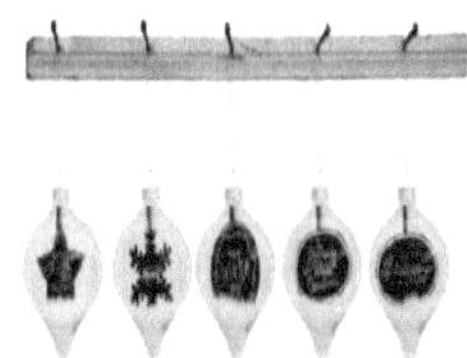

Analysis found no distinguishing characteristics and the object could have been purchased at any craft or hobby supply shop through out the city of London.

The scene was processed for fingerprints but none were found indicating that the scene was either wiped down by the perpetrator or the perpetrator wore gloves during the attack.

In addition, no unidentified DNA or other bodily fluids were identified at the scene.

The medical examiner retrieved a small piece of rubber like material from one of the incisions which was analyzed and found to be a small quantity of latex rubber similar to the material used for Latex rubber gloves. It is therefore assumed the perpetrator wore latex gloves during the attack and that a small piece of a glove became lodged in the wound. It contained no DNA or other indicator from the perpetrator.

The CID team processed the stairs, doorway entrance and outside area around the building with no results.

In a separate one-page report Tom noted that the Cyber Team had attempted to locate the origin of the email message that Ed had received the morning that the body was found but they had come up with inconclusive findings. The IP address had been traced back to a public IP address that could be accessed by anyone if they knew how to hide their address through a proxy server.

Tom proceeded to take the reports and after filling the two routine coffee cups headed back to Ed's office.

"Where you been," grumbled Ed, "Does it take that long to print a report or were you waiting for the paper reports to arrive."

"Just took the opportunity to read them over before I came back." Tom replied.

"Okay lad, then you may as well give me the break down of what you found in those reports and I will check them later."

Tom was well aware that if he tried to summarize the findings that Ed would have a hay day later chewing him out about the conclusions and suppositions that Ed would see as errors on Tom's part so Tom simply dove into reading the report findings out loud.

He showed Ed the photographs of the crime scene and the Christmas ornament and offered no assumptions.

"Well you have shown me that you can read but what do you think and what does all that gibberish about the computer address in the cyber technicians report really mean."

All the information regarding the computer technology was meaningless to Ed and unfortunately above Tom's level of understanding.

They called the cyber technician who explained that a person can sign into what is called a proxy server which assigns that address to the email and basically hides the real Internet provider (IP) address of the sender.

There was no way that they could trace the message back beyond that proxy server so there was no way to locate the sender's computer in order to identify the sender.

After they hung up from the cyber tech Tom continued, "Based on these reports we do not have much in the line of investigative leads. The perpetrator was organized and was wearing some form of protective clothing and gloves based on the lack of any trace evidence and the small fragment of rubber latex found embedded in the wound.

We can not draw any conclusions on whether his choice of Nancy Graves was random or planned as we have nothing at this time to link her to any potential suspects.

I would recommend that we release some of the details to the public to see if the facts trigger any recognition in anyone regarding the plastic sheet, screw hooks and Christmas ornament without releasing detail of the specific wounds or the decorations on the ornament."

"Well that was a fairly good assessment lad and shows you are actually getting better at being a real detective." Ed replied.

"Contact the department media office and have them prepare a statement for release but make sure they pass it by us before they release it along with the name of the victim."

CHAPTER SEVEN

Tom finished his coffee and left Ed's office heading back to his desk to contact the media department. He noted that Ed was reading intently through the printed reports and felt that he had a fifty-fifty chance of being called out for missing something that Ed would latch onto.

After cleaning out his coffee mug he called the media department and went over what the detectives wanted to be stated in the press release. The media department asked if Ed or Tom would be leading the press conference as the police spokesperson.

I'll check with senior detective Ed Morgan and see if he will or if possibly the deputy chief will want to. Tom knew that Ed despised getting up before the press and speaking and Tom was too junior so the like hood would be that the deputy chief would hold the press conference flanked by Ed and Tom. After talking to Ed about leading the press conference who stated an adamant NO Tom contacted the deputy chief who was happy to oblige.

The media department emailed a press release and talking points page and advised they had notified the press that there would be a press conference in the station conference room at 4:00 p.m. that afternoon.

That would allow the news channels to have the story on the evening broadcasts and the newspapers could expand and print for the next morning edition.

At four p.m. sharp Tom and Ed entered the conference room behind the deputy chief who released details of the horrific murder of Nancy graves, age twenty-three sometime between Friday evening and Saturday morning. He described the fact that she had been incapacitated and tortured. He went on to describe the cause of death as suffocation due to the placement of a plastic bag over her head. He concluded by describing the plastic drop sheet, screw hooks and the fact that the victim had been found with a Christmas Tree Ornament placed in her mouth.

The deputy chief advised that a hot line had been set up so that anyone who may have information on the crime or was aware of any individual that may have been seen with these items to contact the police. Copies of the hot line number were distributed to the press.

The deputy chief then opened the press conference to questions but advised there was no further detailed information regarding the case that the police were prepared to release at this time due to the ongoing investigation.

When Tom arrived home that evening and turned on the evening news, he was confronted with the video image of himself and Ed Morgan standing solemnly and somewhat nervously behind the deputy chief while the newscast anchor re iterated the contents of the press conference with the added comment that the police were obviously in the dark regarding the perpetrator of the crime. They showed the hot line number on the bottom of the screen along with "representative" photographs of what the screw hooks and possible Christmas decoration could look like.

The next morning when Tom arrived at the station, he retrieved a copy of the morning London Free Press which had run the story on the front page. In addition to elaborating on the details from the press conference and last nights newscast the newspaper had titled the case as the "Christmas Ornament Killer."

"Tom, coffee and get in here" Ed barked.

Tom filled the coffee mugs and proceeded to go into Ed's office with the morning newspaper tucked under his arm.

"That damn press report makes us look incompetent." Ed snarled, "They expect that we can just look at a crime scene and come up with a clear picture of the perpetrator and have him or her in custody by the end of the first day!"

"Hopefully we get some tangible leads from the hot line and if we do then the information we did not release regarding the mistletoe and the decoration on the ornament can help us nail down a suspect." Tom mused.

"We will just have to wait and see but in the meantime, we have other cases that we need to work on as this is not the only major crime in this forest city."

Tom thought about Ed's comment and the fact that London was known as the Forest City because of the parks and abundance of trees throughout the city limits. This was one of the things that made this city an ideal home as far as Tom and Ann were concerned and why they never choose to relocate back to their hometown of Simcoe.

Tom and Ann used to make the hour and a half drive back to Simcoe on Sunday afternoons to visit both their parents but Toms parents had since passed away and Ann's parents had moved to London to be closer to their grandkids.

The routine now was that every Sunday after attending church at the Maitland street Community of Christ they would all go out for lunch and then visit at Ann's parent's apartment. With the arrival of Kevin, it had become a little harder to find suitable restaurants on Sunday since Kevin generally slept during the class time and service in the nursery room and was awake and fussy during lunch.

AS Tom thought about the upcoming Christmas he recalled that the normal routine for Christmas day at the Grants home had been a quiet morning with just Ann, Tom and Tom Jr getting up and opening their presents before having a family breakfast. Then the family would go over to Ann's parents' home at noon for a Christmas lunch, open more presents and visit. The arrival of Kevin would make the Christmas morning routine a little more chaotic but everyone looked forward to the change.

This year Christmas fell on a Saturday which worked out well since all the stores etc. closed by 6:00 p.m. on Christmas eve and everything stayed close through Christmas Day and Boxing Day celebrated on the 26th.

Tom reflected on the fact that all the US stores were advertising BOXING DAY Sales for the 26th as this was not a statutory holiday in the United States.

Canada followed the British Commonwealth Tradition and boxing day was a holiday with everything closed.

Boxing Day had started in Britain and the theories behind its origins are generally accepted to be one of two that are basically connected to an old tradition of charity where gifts were distributed to the lower classes on the day after Christmas.

The earliest printed reference to the term boxing day was in 1833 and Charles Dickens referred to the day in the "Pickwick papers".

The first theory is that December 26 was the day when the Lords of the manor and aristocrats typically distributed "Christmas boxes" filled with small gifts, money and leftovers from their Christmas dinner to their household servants and employees, who were required to work on December 25th. It was to express recognition for good service throughout the year.

The second theory is that the term boxing day arose from the alms boxes that were placed in churches during the Advent Season for the collection of money donations from parishioners. The clergy would then distribute the content of the boxes to the poor on December 26th which is also referred to as the feast of St Stephen named for the first Christian martyr known for acts of charity.

Tom cherished this time of the year and the way everything went relatively silent for two full days for the major crimes department. Crime rates spiked during the lead up to and over the Christmas season for thefts, fires, and minor disturbances due to a greater degree of "visible" targets with Christmas presents and people travelling to visit family.

Natural Christmas trees were up for nearly a month and if they are not properly watered the dry brittle trees are susceptible to catching fire from Christmas lights.

Domestic disturbances and physical confrontations would spike after Christmas through the New Year Celebrations making Toms former position as a uniformed officer extremely busy.

CHAPTER EIGHT

Tom spent the next few days working on other cases that fell in the jurisdiction of the major crime unit. The members of the major crime section investigated serious and violent crimes including homicides, attempted murder, life-threatening assaults, abduction, and extortions as well as missing persons or found human remains. The department was also tasked with assisting the coroner in the investigation of all sudden deaths except for motor vehicle accidents where no criminality is involved.

Currently he was working with Ed on an assault case where an individual had been hospitalized resulting from a knife attack that occurred in the parking lot of the victim's apartment building. The perpetrator had been identified and apprehended and the department was attempting to identify the motive for the crown attorney.

In addition, Tom and Ed were the lead detectives on a missing person case that was ongoing as the result of a seventeen-year-old girl who had disappeared two weeks earlier. No one was sure if she was abducted or a runaway but the parents were pleading with the girl to come home or the persons who took her to return her so it had become a media driven case.

Ed was of the impression the girl had run off since there was no indication or evidence of foul play and the girl and her mother had a history of arguing. Ed felt this was the result of the teenager rebelling against her mom but the deputy chief had made it very clear that the detectives were not to publicly speculate in that regard.

Tom chuckled to himself because he could see the deputy chief was trying to ensure that Ed did not make his feelings known based on Ed's past tendency to publicly share his thoughts on matters such as this.

Ed was one of the top detectives in the department but also one of the most opinionated.

Tom kept checking in on the hotline that had been established for the missing teenager. They had received unconfirmed reports of sightings of the girl from callers over the past two weeks but none had proved reliable.

Tom opened the file on the missing seventeen-year-old, she lived in a middle-class neighbourhood in west London, no siblings. The report detailed the history of verbal disputes that the girl had with her mother since she turned thirteen. The mother was domineering but did not abuse the girl and the father was described as a mild-mannered individual who preferred to not get involved in the interactions between his wife and his daughter.

It was clearly a dispute between two very opinionated and dominant individuals and the girl disappeared one evening after she had an argument with her mother. She had slammed out of the house with just the clothes she had on at the time, blue jeans, a blue sweater, black toque cap and gloves plus her red winter coat.

The police had canvassed the neighbourhood within hours after the minor age girl became a missing person asking if anyone had seen the girl, any suspicious activity or people in the area.

Everything had turned up negative and there were no reports of anyone seeing the girl. Since there was no evidence to believe the girl had been abducted or in imminent danger the police did not issue an 'Amber" alert.

Forty-eight hours after the disappearance the parents and family members had gone on the news broadcasts showing a picture of their daughter and pleading for information or her return and the news coverage had continued ever since.

Tom took out the photograph from the file which showed a pretty young red haired sixteen-year-old teenager in her school uniform smiling in the picture taken for last years class photos.

In addition, Tom kept checking with the hotline on the Graves murder. They had received calls from individuals claiming they had seen a neighbour or someone else with painters drop cloths or that owned screw hooks but again none of these proved out to be any more then speculation.

One of the callers had stated that she knew who had done it but upon investigating the allegation it turned out to be a jilted girl friend who wanted to get back at her ex.

When Ed and Tom interviewed her, it was clear she had no information outside of what was in the news and it turned out the ex-boyfriend was out of town during the weekend in question travelling with his new companion.

Ed did not hold back in chastising the young lady and letting her know that filing a false police statement was a serious crime that could result in her being charged and if convicted prison time.

The young lady left but based on her attitude it was clear that she was still vindictive and not remorseful for her actions.

"Are we going to charge her?" Tom asked.

"Let's turn the details over to the crown attorney and let him decide." Ed replied.

Nearly sixteen days after the missing person repot was filed on the young girl Ed received a call from the Hamilton Police Department. The girl had been located in Hamilton and staying at the home of another girl she had met online. The other girls' parents had thought she had left home due to family disputes and had not called the police until after she had been staying with their daughter for over two weeks.

The Hamilton police picked up the girl and apparently had a strong discussion with the friend's parents in regard to harboring a runaway minor and not coming forward sooner.

The Hamilton detective who called Ed and Tom told them that the couple stated they thought she was over eighteen based on what she had told them and felt they were simply helping her out. They had seen the news cast and stated that they had been talking to her about the need to contact her parents and when she didn't, they finally decided to notify the authorities that she was at their home.

Later that day the girl arrived at the London police station having been transported from Hamilton by a unformed officer. Her parents had been notified and were waiting in the station when she arrived.

Tom and Ed interviewed the teenager and sternly discussed the fact that she was underage and if she persisted in these actions, she could be placed in a juvenile detention facility for run away minors.

Defiantly she retorted, "I am seven months away from my eighteenth birthday and when that day comes, I can go where I want and neither you nor my mother can do anything about it. I will be an adult."

As the girl left with her parents looking sullen and defiant the detectives debated on whether they would see the girl in a year or two either out on the streets of London or filed as an adult missing person case at that time.

As Ed remarked, "Our job is to work within the law and do what the law dictates, we are not and never will be social workers to address the needs of the individuals when it goes past fulfilling our duty." Tom understood but he felt that as a human and a devout Christian he wished there was more that he could do to help.

CHAPTER NINE

It was snowing softly the evening of Friday December 17th. Sally Bentley was out having a few drinks and a good time with her friends at a bar in St Thomas Ontario. The conversation had been lively as everyone discussed preparations for the upcoming Christmas vacation and the impending New Years Eve celebrations.

The group of long standing friends had gathered at the Bar to listen to music, talk, laugh and generally have a good time together. Of the ten, six were in couple relationships and the other four were between entanglements as they liked to call their current situation.

Sally was one of the four singles as she had broken up with her boyfriend of two years just four months earlier when he decided to accept a job opportunity in western Canada. He had neither discussed his plans of moving to Calgary Alberta with her nor had he asked Sally to come with him.

She was slightly bitter and very disillusioned regarding men at this point in her Twenty-five-year-old journey of life. Not that she would have trouble attracting another attachment since she was blond and petite with a good figure. She was liked by everyone and considered to be the life of the party with her easy laughter and fun attitude. She simply had decided that she was not ready to quickly jump into any re bound relationship after the hurt she had felt from her boyfriend's betrayal.

It was nearly midnight when the group started to wind down the evening and break up to go their sperate ways.

Sally liked the feel of the crisp winter air and the sight of the Christmas lights hanging on the city streetlamp poles, shops, and buildings, so she decided to walk the short distance from the bar to her apartment which was only a ten-minute walk away.

Saying her goodbyes and assuring everyone that she was perfectly safe walking home in the small community of approximately thirty thousand people she had grown up in she set out with her coat hood pulled up to protect her face from the snow. She had made it over halfway home on the deserted streets when suddenly she felt someone grab her from behind. She tried to lash out at the stranger but was overpowered by strong hands as she felt a cloth clasped on her face covering her nose and mouth as she drifted off into unconsciousness.

Sally awoke feeling groggy and confused. She was unable to move her arms or legs as she lay spread eagle on the floor. Her eyes darted around the dimly lit room and rested on a wooden chair against the wall. On the chair was a folded pile of clothing that she recognized as hers which made her come of the sickening realization that she was lying naked on what felt like a plastic sheet.

She tried to scream but her mouth was sealed by a strip of duct tape.

Softly she heard a voice coming from the end of the room and a black clad figure appeared in her line of sight.

"Glad to see you're awake." The figure whispered. "I hope you had fun in the bar. You appeared to be having quite a good time and were the life of the party. That's why I chose you to come here and party with me. Merry Xmas. "

Panic welled up in Sally as she watched the figure moving towards her carrying a scalpel knife that glinted in the dim light. She tried to scream or to move but neither her screams came out nor could she move her arms and legs. Her only movement was to writhe from side to side as the scalpel started to cut into the flesh of her stomach.

The pain was excruciating and after a short period of time Sally succumbed and blissfully drifted into unconsciousness from the panic and the pain.

Sally awoke some time later with her body feeling like it was on fire from the cuts that had been inflicted.

"I've been waiting for you to wake up." The voice said, "So that I can watch when you leave our party."

The duct tape had been removed from Sally's mouth and she desperately pleaded with the dark figure through her pain to let her go. Through her sobs Sally felt the clear plastic bag being slipped over her head. She felt the tightness of the duct tape as it was placed around her neck sealing the air from reaching her nose and mouth. She struggled and gasped in pure terror as the plastic was sucked into her mouth depriving her lungs of air until she again felt her mind pass into oblivion.

Chapter Ten

Monday morning December 20th Tom arrived at the station to begin the work week. It was just five days till Christmas eve and he and Ann were going to the Christmas eve Candlelight service at church. Christmas day would see the routine of Tom Jr opening presents. As he had gotten older the anticipation had gotten higher every year.

Now that Tom Jr was seven, they had decided to re kindle an old tradition in Tom's family regarding the Christmas stocking. Rather then hanging the stocking in the living room when Tom Jr went to bed the stocking was taken into his bedroom on Christmas eve and laid at the end of the bed. During the night "Santa Clause" would come in and fill the stockings with appropriate candies, treats and small gifts that Tom Jr was allowed to open Christmas morning before the main event of opening presents around the Christmas tree.

Tom Sr had never figured out as a young child until after he got older that Santa Clause did not really exist. The reality was that his parents were coming into his room after he was asleep and putting the items into the stocking.

It was such a childhood joy to wake up on Christmas morning and grab the filled stocking from the end of the bed and to open the small gifts, books, treats and items in your bedroom.

The other thing Tom did not realize as a child was that the stocking ritual also allowed his parents to sleep longer as the rule was you could open your stocking gifts and items but not come downstairs to the living room till after six o'clock on Christmas morning after your parents were awake.

Tom always looked forward to Christmas and this time with his young family and with visiting Ann's parents on Christmas Day.

He soon heard Ed's routine bellow to get in here so Tom filled the obligatory two cups of coffee and headed for the office.

"I have another one of those damn emails on my computer in box. Read it." Ed grumbled.

Tom opened Ed's email box and wondered if Ed really did not know how or if he was simply refusing to use the email system. Ed continuously stated that if someone wanted to talk to him the telephone worked just fine rather then trying to decipher those damn electronic messages.

The email was signed 'Santa Clause' and Tom felt a wave of premonition as the email had been sent Saturday afternoon, over thirty-six hours ago.

'Greetings again Detective Morgan. I hope you enjoyed my first present I left for you but you never thanked me and I was watching the news closely. I found it quite refreshing to have a nickname now and you can call me the Christmas Ornament Killer from now on. But this weekend I left you another Xmas gift since we are so close to Christmas. Your present is 'wrapped' and waiting for you in the upstairs of the old factory on the east end of the main street in St Thomas. '

Ed looked at Tom and told him to contact the Deputy Chief. They needed to coordinate the search with the St Thomas police force and Ed wanted to be there when they located the building.

Tom called the Deputy Chief and advised him of the email and its contents and requested that he and Ed proceed to the St Thomas police station and participate in the search. The Deputy Chief agreed and told them to head over and he would contact the St Thomas Chief.

Tom went back to Ed's office and before they left, he forwarded Ed's email to the CID electronic forensics team to see if they could get a trace on the sender or origin from this one as there was no 'return' address to reply to the email.

Tom remembered what the cyber technician had told him last time about proxy servers but he was hoping the perpetrator may have slipped up.

Ed was quiet as they drove the thirty minutes from the London Police Station to the St Thomas station located in the justice building at the corner of

Curtis and St Catherine's streets. The St Thomas police force was composed of forty-six members. Thirty-five constables, eight sergeants, one staff sergeant, the deputy chief and Chief. The force had been in existence since 1852 and had grown to provide a police presence designed to meet the needs of the town of thirty some thousand. In addition, St Thomas had their own Criminal Investigation and forensics team. The larger London Police had assisted the St Thomas force in the past when required with additional resources.

They arrived at the St Thomas station and entered being greeted by the desk receptionist who took them to the deputy chiefs office.

After introductions were made the deputy chief lead Tom and Ed to a conference room and introduced them to the officers who would be the investigating officers at the crime scene if the information was true along with the department Criminal Investigation officer.

Ed briefed the officers on the details of the first homicide two weeks earlier in London and the emails from the perpetrator. They established the fact that London and St Thomas would be conducting a joint investigation at the scene and if the homicide proved to be linked with the first then the London police detectives would be taking over the lead on both cases.

"If this proves out to be the same perpetrator then we are looking at a serial murderer investigation with the potential for more victims occurring." Tom commented.

They left the station heading downtown St Thomas to the closed factory on main street. The St Thomas police had already contacted the realtor who had the property listed for sale in the event they needed assistance entering the building.

When they arrived, they found a back door which had been broken open by splintering the wood around the lock and prying the door open.

The St Thomas officer thanked the Realtor for coming and advised that this was an active crime scene and he would need to remain outside.

When they entered, they proceeded to the closed office located on the factory floor. Fortunately, the electricity was still turned on to the building as the owner had it listed for sale. When they turned on the lights in the office, they were met with the same disturbing sight that Tom and Ed had confronted in London.

Lying naked and staked out with screw hooks and cords on the floor lay the body of a young women approximately twenty-five years old. Her body and the plastic sheet under her were covered with dried blood from the deep gash wounds that covered her body.

The Criminal Investigation Team from St Thomas had arrived and were processing the crime scene. Tom advised them of what items were key from the original crime scene processing. The coroner arrived and examined the body noting that the victim had a small tear shaped Christmas ornament located inside her mouth and bagged it for processing.

Based on the two homicides being linked the coroner stated that his office would contact the London office and coordinate the autopsy.

Tom noted the similarities between the scenes. The perpetrator had carved the words Merry Xmas into the stomach of the victim, folded the clothes neatly on the wooden chair against the wall, hung a sprig of plastic mistletoe from the beam over the victims head, and placed the identical looking Christmas ornament in her mouth post mortem.

The victim was lying on her back on a plastic painter's cloth and was secured by the wrists and ankles with the same type of cord and four screw hooks driven into the floor.

Tom was hopeful that the Criminal Investigation team would find some discarded evidence or fingerprints but based on the history of the prior crime scene the perpetrator had been meticulous in his actions.

Tom and Ed observed the ambulance attendant's removal of the body and provided their contact information to the corner and the criminal Investigation lead. They agreed that they would send copies of their reports to Tom and Ed as this was now a serial killer investigation under the lead of the London Detective Department.

As they left the building, Tom noticed the gathering of reporters who had converged on the site clambering for details and statements.

The St Thomas Police Chief had arrived on the scene and he was conducting a press conference with the media without consulting with the investigating officers.

Ed looked at Tom shaking his head and stated, "Let's get out of here before he tries to pull us into his circus. We will have the opportunity to hear what he is saying on this evening's news."

Tom and Ed said their goodbyes to the attending St Thomas officers and the Deputy Chief and drove back to the London police station.

CHAPTER ELEVEN

The St Thomas police force took on the task of notifying the family of Sally Bentley and following up with the investigation of Sally's movements on the Friday night of the homicide.

When the forensics and autopsy reports arrived Tom and Ed compared them with the print outs from the first Homicide.

Sally Bentley had died from suffocation caused by the securing of a plastic bag over her head cutting off the flow of oxygen to her lungs.

The wounds had been inflicted on her arms, legs, and stomach using a sharp knife or scalpel and had all been inflicted prior to her death.

The two-inch screw hooks driven into the wooden plank floor were identical to the ones used in the first homicide as was the cord used to secure her.

In addition, the mistletoe suspended over her head and the Christmas ornament were a match to the ones utilized in the staging of the Nancy Graves murder.

The scene had been processed by the Criminal Investigative officers and they again had found no fingerprints or body fluids to identify the attacker.

The cyber technician had verified that the perpetrator had again use a proxy server for the email preventing them from identifying the actual computer used.

Ed was still fuming over the press comments made by the St Thomas Police Chief who had told the media that this murder was identical to the London homicide two weeks ago and was obviously the work of a deranged serial killer.

He described the similarities and went so far as to release details of the two murders that the London police had chosen not to make public. His action had hindered Tom and Eds investigation and increased the potential for copycat killings.

In addition the fact that the perpetrator was contacting a detective with the London Police force was also made public.

Since then, the press had been calling the station regularly asking the London Deputy Chief for updates and further information. The news was having a field day of speculation with suppositions stating to the public that the individual was targeting young women in their mid twenties, brutally torturing them and that women should not walk the streets of the city or any nearby cities without protection.

The mayor had also become involved complaining to the London Police Chief that the force needed to make an arrest and put a stop to the negative impact that the publicity was having on the city.

In response to the heightened attention a task force was established, chaired directly by the Deputy Chief and composed of Ed, Tom, two other detectives from London as well as the deputy Chief from St Thomas as a consulting member.

A "war room" had been set up in one of the departments conference rooms displaying evidence boards covered with photos of the crime scenes, the written reports, and the emails. An electronic forensics technician had also been assigned to the room to monitor any communications and electronic activity that may be appearing over the internet.

Tom knew that Ed despised the electronic age but the fledgling world wide web and internet service providers that had emerged in the 1980's had resulted in a revolutionary impact on culture, commerce, and technology including the rise of near instant communications by electronic mail. Email had come into being in the 1970's and was now a major form of communication.

The internet or world wide web was a new area of investigation that was becoming more and more a must for the policing services as new methods of using the web began to surface.

The dedicated telephone tip line was located in the war room for people to call regarding any information they might have.

The one main advantage that Tom saw with the establishment of the task force was that he now had a desk located in the war room where he could bring his cup of coffee while he worked.

The task force's main function was to sort through the hot line calls that had grown exponentially with the second homicide and the new reports.

The police were getting hundreds of calls from people reporting 'suspicious' acting individuals who they believed were following them in the evenings. Each report of a suspicious person or a neighbour who was observed carrying paint-ers' cloths or tools had to be investigated and ruled out by the force.

After spending all week after the second homicide including the Friday of Christmas eve the department and the mayor's office were on edge in antici-pation for the following Monday morning concerned whether another email would arrive for Ed from the killer.

The Christmas weekend remained quiet regarding the christmas ornament killer and the task force breathed a sigh of relief.

Tom had spent Christmas eve with his family at the candlelight service at church but his mind kept going back to the two homicides.

Nancy had been out celebrating her birthday with a couple of friends at a local wine bar. There was no party to attract attention but the killer had targeted her when she was walking home. Sally had been at a bar for a pre-Christmas party with a small group of friends. Again, the party had not been loud or bois-terous to attract attention but she had been targeted walking home. Nancy was not involved with anyone and had no romance related disputes while Sally had broken up with her partner and had no current romantic interest. In addition, her former boy friend was provinces away in Alberta during the time of the homicide in question.

The only link that seemed to stand out was that they had both been attacked while walking home from spending the evening in a bar leading Tom to assume the perpetrator was choosing his victims at random when his target left the bar. How he knew they were walking was a mystery unless he picked different individuals of the same basic age etc. and observed them from outside the bars as they left walking alone.

No one had been identified hanging around inside the bars acting suspicious so Tom considered the fact that he or she was waiting outside made the most sense. He wondered if the task force should re interview patrons from the two locations and see if anyone noticed someone who was in the vicinity outside the bar on the nights in question. He knew it was a long shot but the best he could come up with.

Christmas morning and Christmas day went as planned with Tom Jrs delight on finding his Christmas stocking on the end of his bed filled with items. He had been kept busy in his bedroom involved with the stocking till after six a.m. before he woke up his baby brother by 'whispering' to him that it was Christmas morning.

After the ritual of the presents being opened and breakfast completed the family got dressed and went over to the grandparents where Tom Jr opened his gifts from his grandparents.

CHAPTER TWELVE

After the Christmas holidays ended the task forces full attention continued for the next full week through to New Years Eve with no significant breaks, leads, or creditable information.

Tom, Ed and the St Thomas task force officers followed up on the suggestion from Tom going back to the two bars identified as the starting place for the abductions to find the patrons who were in those establishments on the evenings in question. The task was not easy but those they were able to locate all stated that they had not noticed or paid any attention to who may have been outside the bars when they left those nights.

One individual did remember seeing a man standing in the entrance to a closed store across the street from the wine bar in London but he assumed he was a homeless individual and did not pay much attention to what he looked like. All he could remember was that he was average height, well built but not overweight and was wearing a black toque hat and a long trench coat.

Monday morning of the third week after the second homicide the task force continued to meet thankful that no email had arrived from the perpetrator proclaiming another victim.

The follow up on potential leads continued into the third week but the detectives were also assigned to other cases on a part time basis to better utilize police resources. For the benefit of the press and public the station media spokesperson maintained that a dedicated task force was working diligently on the Christmas Ornament Homicides.

On the Thursday morning of the third week, Tom was assigned to partner with a uniformed officer and investigate a family dispute that had turned violent when a young man had stabbed his brother and father in a domestic dispute.

When they arrived at the home where the altercation took place the mother was visibly agitated and demanded that her son be arrested and locked up for attempted murder.

Tom tried to calm her down so he could ask her questions regarding the dispute. Emergency Measures Technicians (EMTs) had arrived and were providing medical attention to what appeared to be minor wounds that had been inflicted on the assailant's father and brother. The suspect was in custody and sitting handcuffed in the back of a police cruiser at the scene.

Tom asked the mother:" Can you describe what happened and how the dispute started?"

"Edward went crazy when my husband told him he needed to get his belongings and get out of our house, he is not going to school or working, just living off us."

"How old is your son."

"He's fifteen years old and nothing more then a lazy bum."

Tom noted the fact that the perpetrator was a minor which meant that he would need to ensure an advocate was contacted to come to the station before he interviewed the boy. It was obvious that the parents would not be coming to participate in the interrogation

The Father came over to where Tom and his wife were talking. Tom noted that the EMTs had bandaged the wound on his right hand and lower arm.

Tom introduced himself, showed his credentials and asked the gentleman to describe what had taken place.

"My son came home and I met him at the door. He turned fifteen the end of August and dropped out of school at the start of the school year. He is not willing to go back to school or get a job. I have told him repeatedly that he needs to make a positive move regarding his life choices or I was not going to support him. If he wanted to live under my roof he needed to abide by my rules.

Its been getting tenser over the past few weeks and last weekend he went out Friday afternoon for New Years eve He never showed up at home till late in the afternoon of new years day.

I told him that this was unacceptable behaviour.

Last night he didn't show up again till this morning and I met him at the door. I told him that we have had enough and that he was to pack up his clothes and find someplace else to live. The discussion turned into a yelling match and our younger son tried to intervene. Our younger son pushed his brother. Edward pulled a knife and lashed out at him. I got in between them and he slashed my hand and arm with the knife.

My wife had called the police while we in the front yard arguing and when my younger son again got involved Edward slashed my younger son's shoulder with the knife.

The police arrived and my son tried to run away but the police officers caught him and brought him back to their cruiser in handcuffs."

Tom asked if he could talk with the younger son.

The boy was approximately thirteen and visibly shaken and distraught.

"Can you describe what happened." Tom queried.

"Edward just went nuts. He was arguing with my Dad and they were both angry. I tried to stop them and then Edward pulled a knife. I have never seen him act like that before. He attacked my dad and me with the knife."

"Did you observe the dispute between your father and your brother."

"Sure. Dad told him he needed to collect his stuff from our room and to move out. They then started yelling at each other and my brother attacked my dad."

Tom talked with the EMT's who advised the wounds were minor in nature and they had been bandaged but the two should get medical attention in case of infection.

Tom advised the uniformed officers to take the older son to the station and arrange for an advocate to be in the interview room when he returned.

He then went into the house and continued the discussion with the family. The mother was adamant that she wanted the boy charged for assaulting his father and brother but the father was calmer and more rational asking if there was any way that his son may be able to get help as he was not willing to allow him to come back home. He stated the safety of his wife and younger son were the most important considerations but he did not want to see his boy end up on the streets and get into more serious trouble.

Tom advised them that it would be up to the crown attorney regarding charges but he would be treated as a juvenile because of his age. A Children's Aid Society representative would be contacting them shortly to discuss options moving forward.

"I don't want him coming back here!" The mother proclaimed.

"The children's aid society worker will discuss with you what is available and if Edward can not be returned home, they will determine the need for a protection agreement and arrange with you to retrieve his belongings."

Tom was thinking to himself, if the young man had no criminal record and this was a first offense then the crown attorney would not push for Edward to be charged and sentenced to a juvenile facility.

Children's aid society services would talk with the parents and see if they could arrange for counselling with the intent of re-establishing a family relationship and if not, Edward would need to be placed in alternative housing such as a relative, friend, group home or similar facility.

Chances of foster parents willing to take in a fifteen-year-old was a short-term possibility. Children and youth in the Children's services system were maintained by the system until they "aged out" when they turn sixteen and are classed as an adult.

At that point the 'adult' you would be basically on their own with little support or services provided so the reality was that Edward could end up on the street or collecting welfare assistance.

The only exception is if the youth and the children's aid society make a written agreement for services and support where:

- The society has jurisdiction over where the child resides
- The society has determined that the child is or may be in need of protection

- The society is satisfied that no course of action less disruptive to the child, such as care in the child's own home or with a relative, neighbour or other member of the child's community or extended family is able to adequately protect the child, and
- The child wants to enter into the agreement.

Tom was aware that youth the age of Edward often refused services under the system because they do not want to meet the requirements for attending school or being controlled which meant they generally end up homeless on the streets.

Tom felt it was a shame that society was so easily willing to simply throw off kids at age sixteen which meant that, if fortunate they received help from other social groups or they drift into the legal system often turning to drugs which was becoming a growing problem in the community.

Tom and the uniformed officer returned to the station where Edward along with a worker from the Children's Aid Society were waiting in an interview room.

Edward was sitting staring at his hands folded in his lap and even though he was projecting a defiant attitude Tom could see that the tears were not far from his eyes. Tom's heart ached at the sight of the young man but he also knew that the youth was now part of the justice system.

"Hello, my name is Detective Tom Grant," and he showed his credentials to Edward and the social worker. "I need to ask you questions about what happened at your parents' home."

"Nothing much happened." Edward responded. "We had a fight."

"Can you tell me what led up to the fight?"

"My mom was upset because I stayed out last night at a friends house. She is always yelling at me and picking at me no matter what I do."

"Did you drop out of school this past fall?"

"Sure, school is of no value and its boring. I told them I wouldn't go any more."

"Describe the events that lead up to you using the knife on your father and brother?"

"My mom was yelling at me so I walked out of the house. My dad followed me and he was shouting that I needed to get my belongings and move out. My brother pushed me so I pulled the knife. I guess I slashed my brothers' shoulder but I didn't mean to. I just wanted him to back off."

"And your father?"

"Dad pushed in between us and I started to trip backwards. I guess the knife cut my dad on the arm and hand as I stepped back. I saw the police cruiser and I ran but the police caught me. They handcuffed me and put me in the cruiser."

"Have you ever gotten into a physical altercation with your family before."

"Not physical but they were always picking on me, telling me what to do."

"I am going to talk to the crown attorney and your family to see if they wish to press charges, in the meantime I am going to release you to the children's aid society worker if you are willing to follow their rules and requirements and if the Children's Aid Society agrees.

I am going to file this report with the crown attorney while you and the social worker discuss your options. I will come back and let you know the outcome with the crown attorney."

Tom left the interview room and went back to his desk where he typed up the report. He called the crown attorney and discussed the circumstances of the case as well as emailing over the report. The crown attorney agreed that they would not lay charges under the circumstances if the father was agreeable.

Tom called Edwards' father and they talked about the case. The father agreed he would not press charges and he agreed to speak on behalf of his younger son as they did not want Edward to have a criminal record for assault. He asked what would happen and Tom explained that Edward would be under the Children's Aid Societies care and they would be contacting the family for discussion and to establish a go forward plan.

Tom returned to the conference room.

"The crown attorney is not going to proceed as your father has agreed not to press charges for the assault. You will not be allowed to go home so you will need to go with the children's aid society worker and she will make the arrangements for where you will be staying and discuss your options. Do you have any questions?"

Edward simply shook his head No but Tom could sense that he was again close to breaking down. He looked so young and lost Tom hoped that the Children's Aid Society would be able to work with the family and patch up their differences but he realized the outcome was unsure.

CHAPTER THIRTEEN

Throughout the balance of the week the task force continued to meet and sort through the catalogued evidence and any potential leads from the hot line. CID had analyzed the small piece of black rubber found on the first victim, Nancy Graves and had identified it as the material used to make black scuba gloves which lead to the assumption the perpetrator was possibly wearing a full scuba body suit during the attacks. That would explain the total lack of any fingerprints, hairs, sweat or other body fluid identification evidence that could have provided a link to the individual's DNA.

The key realization based on this assumption is that the perpetrator was preparing the crime scenes before he obtained his victims since he would be conspicuous walking around in a black scuba suit. That left the team targeting the only possible evidence they could have would be on the victims outer clothing during the abduction.

The police were aware that the perpetrator was using a cloth with ether like material to incapacitate the victim and would be wearing gloves but possibly there may be some other evidence on the victims' outer garments.

Ed called the CID and asked them to re process the victims outer clothing based on their theory and see if something developed.

It was Friday January 7th[th] at 5:00 p.m. when Tom and Ed decided to pack up the office for the weekend and prepared to head to their homes.

Tom checked his phone and listened to a message left by the London free press asking if he, as an investigating detective on the Christmas ornament killer would be willing to contact the reporter and provide an interview. The reporter stated that she felt it would be a good precaution for a detective on the case to advise women what they should be doing to protect themselves.

Tom called the reporter back and told her that all information regarding the case was to be released through the departments media office and he had nothing to add.

"But Detective Grant. Can you not provide some advice for our readers how they should protect themselves from this mad man?"

"The best information is to advise your readers to not go walking at night alone, stay in groups and not make yourself a potential isolated target. In addition, the investigation has not verified if the suspect is male or female at this point."

The reporter thanked Tom for his comments and Tom left the police station.

Tom spent the weekend trying to recuperate from the stresses of the job and the holiday season. The baby was having a bout of teething and croup that was keeping both him and Ann up during the nights. Tom jr had received a toboggan from his grandparents for Christmas and was adamant that he wanted to be outside all day Saturday in the snow and with Ann tending to Kevin it fell on Tom to oblige his oldest son.

The small hill that they went to seemed like a mountain to Tom jr. He would toboggan down the hill screaming and laughing in delight before Tom would have to help him pull the toboggan back to the top. The hill was crowded with other young ones doing the same activity and Tom was one of several parents who had to trudge to the top of the hill and then trudge back down to meet their child at the bottom only to trudge back up again.

After an hour Tom succeeded in getting Tom Jr to agree to head home with the promise of hot chocolate and cookies.

Tom thought about their new home and his young family and was thankful. He vowed to never allow his family to get estranged enough that his children would fall into the same problems as young Edward who he had met this past week.

Being a family is hard work and Tom was committed to make sure he did everything that was needed.

On Sunday morning the Grant family went to the Maitland Community of Christ church as usual. On this morning the congregation was having a business meeting after the eleven o'clock service to discuss a request from the Thames Valley School Board that owned the property next to the church.

It appeared that the school board had approached the church Pastor regarding the boards need to build a sports center adjacent to their sport field complex next store and wanted to purchase the church building.

The Pastor and his counsellors along with the church's London District President and Bishop had met with the school board representatives and were coming back to the congregation with the school boards proposal.

"To begin I would like to thank the congregation for staying after the service in order to hold this congregational meeting. I realize that this is cutting into your Sunday afternoon social time of coffee and refreshments that we normally host in the fellowship hall." stated the Pastor.

"The Thames Valley District School Board approached us last month and requested that we consider an offer from the school board to purchase our church building.

The offer entails the school board obtaining our building for the sum of one and a half million dollars as well as donating back to us a piece of property owned by the school board on Colborne street which is suitable to build a new church home.

The school board will be tearing down this building in order to build a sports complex as part of the adjacent sports field the school currently owns.

Since the building is to be torn down the school board has agreed that we are welcome to remove any items we wish from our current church home and install them in the new church. We have discussed the fact that we want to have the large stain glassed windows here in the sanctuary taken out and re installed in the new sanctuary along with the pews we currently own."

Tom gazed around the sanctuary looking at the two large stained-glass windows that had been installed when the church had been built in 1916. The one referred to as the Good Shepherd window displayed the image of Christ as the shepherd with his flock.

The other was donated in 1916 in memory of individuals within the congregation.

The Bishop then took over the meeting and asked if there were any questions regarding the proposal before he called for a motion. Members of the congregation rose to ask questions.

'What would the new church home look like?"

'My family built this church and how can we simply see it torn down?'

'What is the condition of this building since it is over eighty years old, are we facing major renovations and repairs?'

"My mother had to stop attending church here in this building even thought she loved it because the stairs to come up to the sanctuary are simply to much for her.'

After the Pastor and Bishop responded to the questions verifying that the new church would be build so that it is handicap accessible in all areas, that a committee would be elected to work with the architect on the design and that the membership would have full input into how the church should be built and the look of the building.

After a lengthy discussion the congregation was moving past the nostalgia for the building and started to discuss the potential for growth and mission that a new congregational home could provide at which point the Bishop asked for a motion.

It was one of the oldest and longest-term members of the congregation who rose. Albert was ninety-five years old and stated.

"I have been a member of this congregation since I was a child and my family were part of the congregation when it was built and they moved into this building. But if we are to be followers of Christ we need to move past the bricks and mortar of a building and move forward so we are equipped to meet the needs around us. It is with both sadness and a sense of hope that I rise to move that the Maitland Street congregation accept the offer of purchase and that we establish a committee to oversee the construction of a new church home."

The motion was seconded and after a small discussion the motion was passed unanimously.

The Pastor then asked for nominations to a ten-member committee to oversee the construction of the new church home. The Pastor and counsellors would be ex officio along with the Bishop so they needed to elect six others from the membership.

Nominations were opened and Tom Grant was one of those nominated.

Tom looked around the sanctuary and when asked he accepted to have his name stand which resulted in him being elected as a member of the new church building committee.

After the meeting adjourned the members of the congregation were in no hurry to leave the sanctuary but simply sat and talked in the atmosphere of their beloved church home.

The new construction would take two years to complete so the congregation would continue to meet in this building until it was time to take out the stained-glass windows, pews etc. to be placed into storage until the new home was ready for them to be installed. When that time came the congregation were determined to arrange a final service and then meet in an alternate location temporarily until the new church home was complete.

Congregants gathered in small groups and mingled together to discuss the path forward realizing that the time of fellowship and worship in this building would be limited. Everyone understood that this transition would be a time of nostalgia and contemplation but also, I time of vision and dreaming towards the future.

The Pastor asked the newly elected members of the building committee to join him in the office for a quick planning discussion to set the path forward. Tom left Ann tending to Tom jr and Kevin while she met with the other mothers in the nursery as he prepared to embark on a new volunteer adventure.

Chapter Fourteen

It was two o'clock in the afternoon of January 8th when Peter Cassidy woke up alone in his bed, stretched and prepared to meet the rest of the day. Waking up alone was not new, it had been his lifelong routine since he was born on march twenty fifth, nineteen thirty-four at the hospital in the City of London.

His mother died in childbirth and there was no record of who his father was so Peter began his life in the foster home system being passed from one temporary home to another until he was five years of age.

At age five Peter was adopted by a young married couple, Casey and Albert Cassidy who lived in a small farm on the outskirts of Allenford, just north of London. Peter had spent his fifty-nine years of life never travelling farther away then five hundred miles from his place of birth.

He went into the bathroom to take a shower and stood staring at the scars that covered his arms, legs and stomach in the mirror. The deep rooted feelings of being seen as a freak and the impotence he had suffered since he was twelve had meant that he had never had an intimate relationships with any one.

He had arrived home at four a.m. this morning and proceeded into the barn to hang up his black rubber scuba diving suit from the beam that suspended the suit over the drain in the structures single horse stall. He washed the suit down with the water hose so that the remains of the blood would be carried away into the septic tank in the back yard. He knew that the septic system enzymes would break down the blood the same as it broke down the sewage from the house and disperse it over the septic weeping tile field buried behind the barn.

Peters' adoption in 1939 had began simple enough and he had been part of a relatively normal family until nineteen forty-three when his life turned into a series of torture and pain.

The second world war had started the year he was adopted and Albert Cassidy had enlisted in the Canadian army shortly after the attack on Pearl harbour on December seventh, nineteen forty-one when the Japanese had bombed the naval base and forced the United States into the war.

Albert died in action in nineteen forty-three when Peter was nine.

Following the death of her husband Carey had started to drink heavily, living on a war widows' pension from the Canadian government veterans affairs department since she was unable to work as the result of a mental condition that Carey suffered that was never properly diagnosed and treated.

Combined with the drinking Carey turned mean and spiteful towards the world and particularly towards Peter. It started with small things at first like sending him to his room without meals, sticking him in the legs and arms with pins, scalding his back in the bathtub with hot water.

Peter never told anyone at school about what was happening because Carey would yell at him and tell him if he told anyone she would say he was lying and hurting himself. She would make sure that he spent the rest of his life in an asylum, locked up in a padded room. She told him wild stories of what the doctors and nurses would do to him in those places.

When Peter was twelve years old Casey had taken him out to the barn three weeks before Christmas. In the old horse barn, she had stripped him naked, laid him on his back on the floor and tied his wrists and ankles to the support beams of the stall so that he was spread eagle on the floor. She gagged Peters mouth with a cloth so he couldn't talk or scream. Carey had then proceeded to lash him with a leather razor Strap that had been used by her deceased husband to sharpen his straight razor. The edge of the strap gouged lines into his arms, legs and stomach cutting deep wounds that bled.

In his mind Peter silently begged her to stop until he had sunk into unconsciousness.

Carey left him on the floor for several hours as he drifted in and out of consciousness.

When she returned, she was drunk and dancing around the barn singing Christmas Carols. She hung a sprig of mistletoe on the beam above Peter's head and kissed him on the forehead laughing.

Carey left again but came back with a pail of hot water and proceeded to pour the scalding water over Peters lower stomach and genitals. Peter again passed out from the excruciating pain.

When he awoke again Carey was sitting on a stool next to him and the gag had been removed from his mouth.

"Awake finally." She giggled.

She was holding a small tear drop shaped tinsel Christmas tree ornament in her hand twirling it between her fingers.

"Merry Christmas to you." She sang to the tune of Happy Birthday.

Carey then took the tinsel ornament and crushed it into small pieces in her hands and then forced the pieces into Peter's mouth. She put a funnel between his lips and poured water down his throat.

"There, now you will always have Christmas to be part of you." Casey laughed

Casey untied Peter and took him into the house keeping him home from school for the balance of the fall term. The pain over Christmas was terrible as his wounds slowly healed leaving him permanently scarred and impotent.

It had taken several weeks over the Christmas school holiday for the wounds to heal into angry scars before Peter was able to return to school.

Peter continued to live in that house for four more years, the cruelty had not stopped after that Christmas and Carey would still go out drinking and disappeared for days at a time.

Peter tried to mentally block out what had happened. He was proficient at school getting good grades even though he was withdrawn and made no friends.

As soon as he turned sixteen Peter packed up what belongings he had and moved out getting a part time job at a local feed store while he finished high school.

At age nineteen he was offered a job at a local funeral home as an ambulance attendant.

The ambulance service was a private service that operated as sidelines for funeral homes, furniture stores, taxis, and towing companies. Even though some individuals argued that providing ambulance services by funeral homes was a serious conflict of interest for the funeral director it was an accepted practice and their involvement was seen as a commitment to provide a much-needed community service. In addition, the funeral home vehicle was often the only equipment in the town capable of comfortably transporting patients in a prone position.

Funeral homes were already staffed, had twenty-four hour a day telephone answering service, and the staff's education in the natural sciences was considered second only to that of the local physician.

Even though no external formal training was available Peter was trained by the funeral home to perform the duties involved.

Peter never contacted his "mother" after he left home until three weeks before the Christmas of nineteen sixty. He felt compelled to drive out to the farm on that Friday evening and knocked on the old farmhouse door. Carey answered the door, half drunk. She was now forty years of age but her appearance looked much older highlighting the signs of a hard life.

"What are you doing here." She snarled. "Come to wish me a Merry Xmas, Christmas Boy."

Peter followed her into the kitchen as she swayed and stumbled in front of him.

Peters' eyes were drawn to a pile of clear plastic bags on the table. He slowly picked up a bag and walked up behind Casey, pulling the bag over her head and holding it tight around her throat.

Carey tried to struggle but in her drunken state she was no match for Peter and could not release herself from his grasp. As she fell towards the floor Peter took her head and slammed it against the edge of the kitchen table.

He saw the blood flowing from her wound as he watched the life drain from her eyes.

Peter checked her pulse to ensure she was dead, removed the plastic bag and any sign that he had been there before he left.

He knew that when she was discovered the assumption would be that she had tripped in her drunken stupor and died from the wound on her head.

On the following Saturday morning she was found by a fuel oil delivery driver who had come to fill the fuel oil tank. The police came to Peter's apartment to inform him of his "mothers" death which had been ruled as accidental just as Peter had predicted.

As the only listed heir and family member Peter inherited the farm and he moved into the farmhouse and his old room where he continued to live from then on.

Over the years the role, training and ownership of the ambulance service had evolved.

In nineteen sixty-six Dr Norman McNally a retired army surgeon was hired by the province of Ontario to *"ensure the development throughout Ontario of a balanced and integrated system of ambulance services..."* establishing standardized training for all ambulance staff.

The *"Fundamentals of Casualty Care"* course was a four week, one-hundred-and-sixty-hour training course taught at Canadian Forces Base Borden near Barrie, Ontario.

Peters employer had sent him to attend that training course so he continued to be employed in the ambulance services.

He again took update training throughout the nineteen seventies with the creation of community college training programs for ambulance service and specialized advanced paramedic training.

Peter had been recognized for his abilities to react calmly in the face of horrific accident scenes and when assisting victims.

Peter was a senior ambulance attendant and Emergency measures Technician by the time he reached his late fifties and he had been to a number of homicide and accidental death scenes that were attended by the London Detective Ed Morgan.

He had once tried to joke with Detective Morgan by stating that they always seemed to meet over dead bodies but the detective had been extremely dismissive and basically ignored Peters remarks.

Peter had few friends and no relationships with women over his fifty-nine years of life due to the scars that covered his body and the reality the night in December nineteen forty-six, so long ago had left him impotent.

Being an ambulance attendant had kept the demons buried within him all those years since the experiences of his childhood. Seeing the pain, suffering and death of those he attended too every day had been enough the keep the internal desires to lash out trapped deep within his consciousness.

October nineteen ninety-three had suddenly changed all that for him.

Peter had entered a small hardware store in St Mary's on his day off just to browse. On a sale shelf he found a package of Christmas decorations marked half price. When he picked up the box of six small tear drop shaped Christmas tree ornaments his mind had been flooded with the memories of that Christmas when he had been twelve years old.

He bought the box and took it home to the farmhouse not really understanding why.

Over the course of that October the demons in his mind had started to build the vision of how he would repay Carey for what she had done by striking out at other women who were just like her.

Chapter Fifteen

Peter took out the polaroid picture of the third victim from the night before and placed it on the wall in the back-bedroom which had been his mothers. Four pictures now lined the wall space above the bed. His mother Carey along with the pictures of Nancy Graves, Sally Bentley and Samantha Jenkins.

Peter thought back to the past two months.

He had taken his time going to different hardware stores, picking up the items he would need.

The cord and plastic drop clothes he had purchased at a hardware store in Simcoe Ontario and the screw hooks from a hardware store in London's east end.

The plastic mistletoe had been the last item he bought at a chain branded craft and floral store.

In November he had located the abandoned warehouse in the east end of London and had observed it for several evenings to ensure that no homeless people were squatting in the building. One night he had succeeded in entering the building without leaving any visible damage and searched out the interior rooms.

That's when he had located the small room in the upstairs second level with old wooden plank floors that would be easy to turn the screw hooks into with a pipe wrench.

The next was to identify the individual who would satisfy his demons.

He knew that she needed to be in her mid twenties and frequent a bar. He really didn't care who she was or how much she drank so long as she fit the image he wanted to punish.

Peter had noticed the small wine bar located in downtown London and a dimly lit alleyway just up the block.

He packed his kit and placed it in the back of his Van. It included a black rubber scuba diving suit he had bought years ago with the intention of someday taking a trip and learning to scuba dive which had never materialized.

In addition, he added one of the painter's plastic drop clothes, four screw hooks, a pipe wrench, and cord.

Finally, in the glove compartment he placed one of the Christmas ornaments, a sprig of plastic mistletoe and an old scalpel he had saved instead of disposing it from work.

In the pocket of his long black coat was a gauze cloth and a bottle of Di-ethyl Ether he took from an open hospital medicine lockup cabinet during the confusion surrounding a hectic period when several individuals came into the hospital by ambulances at the same time.

He pulled a black toque down over his hair and wore surgical gloves as he stood on the Friday evening in the shadows of the closed store front entrance and waited.

Just past eleven he saw a young girl in her twenties come out of the bar with three other girls and they stood and talked at the entrance to the bar. Eventually one of them started to walk down Richmond street heading in his direction as the others waited on the side of the curb.

Peter watched as a Taxi pulled up and left with the other girls and the one, he had now chosen continued to walk towards him. He slipped out of the store doorway and moved to the entrance of the alleyway where his vehicle was parked next to the curb.

Peter had prepared a gauze cloth pad with the ether and as Nancy walked in front of the alley, Peter stepped quietly out behind her and grabbed her from be-hind with his arm around her neck covering her mouth and nose with the cloth.

Taken by surprise she had not had time to struggle or fight back before she collapsed into the drug induced sleep from the anesthetic.

The second time, Peter had chosen to go to the adjacent town of St Thomas. He had noticed the closed factory that was up for sale on one of his ambulance runs and the building had seemed to call out to him.

He had again spent several evenings driving by and watching the building to see if there were any signs of homeless residents or security guards. He did notice a security guards vehicle drive up to the front door and check to ensure it was locked before driving away. That meant they were only doing routine external checks and not patrolling the inside.

As one final check Peter had broken into the building by picking the lock on the back door and walked through to a small office on the old production floor before quickly leaving and re locking the back door. He waited to see if there was a silent alarm which would result in the police arriving at the building.

After an hour of no activity, he was satisfied and set his plan in motion for that Friday evening.

Again, he packed the items into his van that he would need and drove to St Thomas parking in an dark spot in beside a closed store. He had picked out a bar that was a few blocks up the street as the site from which his next target would appear.

At eleven thirty he saw a young lady in her mid twenties emerge from the bar and start to walk down the street towards his van. The snow was falling heavier and he watched as she pulled her coat hood up around her head.

Peter had disengaged the interior lights on his van and he quietly stepped out and stood against the side of the store until he observed Sally Bentley pass him in the darkness. For the second time Peter stepped out and reached around the subject's neck with one arm covering her mouth and nose with the gauze cloth until she too sank into the anesthetic induced sleep.

It only took him a moment to load her into the back of the van and drive across town to the closed factory. He parked the van behind the building and entered through the back door.

He left his coat and toque in the van before he carried Sally into the office wearing his scuba diver suit and protective gloves. He then proceeded methodically to remove the items from his backpack.

Peters first act was to remove all of Sally's clothing which he folded neatly on a wooden chair at the side of the room. He unfolded the plastic painter's cloth in the middle of the floor and laid her naked limp body on the cloth.

The next step was to tie lengths of cord to her wrists and ankles to measure the distance required for the screw hooks. It had required all of his strength in order to drive the screw hooks into the wooden floor by turning the pipe wrench but when all four were secure Peter tied the free ends of the cord to the screw hooks.

Sally was now stretched out spread eagle on the plastic cloth on the floor and peter finished his preparations by hanging the plastic mistletoe above her head from the roof beam before he settled down on the floor against the wall and waited for her to re awaken so the 'fun' could begin.

He had seen the news articles where they had labelled him the Christmas Ornament Killer which had strangely pleased him so he used that title in his second email that he sent to Detective Ed Morgan informing him of the location.

He had not realized when he took the community college classes on using computers and computer programming that the knowledge he had learned would be useful. That allowed him to send the detective the messages without anyone being able to trace them back to him.

I trust the great London police Detective Ed Morgan is willing to listen to me now, he proclaimed to himself.

Last night Peter had taken revenge on his third victim Samantha Jenkins.

He had noticed the abandoned storage building on Longwood Road . Talbotville was a small community that was part of the greater city of London located on Colonel Talbot Road that ran from London to St Thomas.

Peter again spent several nights going to the building and watching to ensure no one was entering or leaving during the night hours. Like before he went to the building and picked the lock in order to enter to ensure there were no alarms or security. After satisfying himself that the site was unattended he located a room that had been used for storage and had a wooden plank floor.

His choice of Bars had changed to a location of a more run-down establishment in the downtown of London that had a clientele that was generally from the poorer segment of society. He had decided it was time to choose someone who was even more like his 'mother' regarding her drinking habit.

He again parked his van inside the entrance to a darkened alleyway between two buildings that was used for deliveries. He waited observing individuals who would come and go to the bar through out the evening and at midnight the bar started to empty out as it was getting close to the end of evening and last call.

Most individuals were walking in groups or walking the other direction until one young lady came out alone and started to stagger up the street towards where Peter was standing in the shadows. She was singing softly in a drunken tone as she wandered up the street. Peter watched to see if anyone else would come out of the bar and follow her along the darkened street but she was alone.

When she managed to walk past where Peter was waiting, he reached out and pulled her into the alleyway covering her mouth and nose with the gauze covered ether. She struggled only slightly before she went limp.

Peter hoped that he had not used too much ether based on her intoxication but all he could do was wait and see. He drove to the abandoned storage building and went through his normal ritual of taking Samantha inside and stripping the clothes from her limp body which he folded neatly on a wooden stool he had found.

The wooden planks of the hard wood floor proved more resistant to the screw hooks then the previous two instances but with hard work he was able to drive home the screw hooks so they were firmly fixed into the floor.

It was nearly two in the morning when Samantha started to come too from the ether sleep and squirmed around in the spread-eagle position she was affixed in on the floor.

Peter's mind filled with a sense of anger and hate as he remembered himself waking up on the floor of the barn horse stable and the complete panic of helplessness it entailed.

"Hello." Peter whispered. "I know this must be uncomfortable but I want you too know that this is only the start of the sensations you will be feeling tonight."

He stared into Samantha's eyes as he showed her the scalpel blade and let the dull edge of the cool metal sweep across her cheek. Samantha gagged and moved convulsively in fear as he sang softly to the tune of Happy Birthday to you, "Merry Christmas to you, Merry Christmas to you, Merry Christmas dear Carey. Merry Christmas to you."

Samantha's mind wanted desperately to shout out that she was not Carey and that he had the wrong person but she was unable too only gag through the duct tape sealing her mouth.

Peter pointed to the Mistletoe hanging above her head and said: "I would like to put a kiss on your forehead but we both know I can't do that. We do not want to leave any saliva evidence for the police to find now do we."

Peter took the scalpel and placed the point of the blade against her stomach and started to methodically cut deep wounds into her stomach wall.

Samantha's mind filled with panic and pain as the stinging cut of the blade continued across her stomach and then along her arms and legs.

Fortunately, she passed into unconsciousness from the pain and when she awoke her whole body felt like it was on fire from the multiple cuts.

She realized that the tape was no longer on her face so she yelled out, "Help me. Somebody help me." Through her sobs and her tears.

"Now that's no way to behave, "Peter remarked, "Don't worry I am going to let you rest very soon."

"Why are you doing this to me," she sobbed.

"Come now Mother, you know very well why. Its just to give to you what you gave to me."

"I am not your mother, I don't know who you are. Please let me go." She pleaded.

Slowly peter placed the plastic bag over her head and whispered, "Hush, it will all be over soon."

Samantha tried to twist her head away from the plastic bag but it continued down over her face, she felt the bag being tightened around her throat with tape.

As the plastic was sucked into her mouth and blocked off her nose and airways the last words she heard were, "Merry Xmas!"

Peter sat on the floor and stared at the dead body of Samantha Jenkins as she lay motionless on the floor. He slowly took out the Christmas ornament from the knapsack where he had placed it beside the door frame and moved over to remove the tape from around her neck.

Gently he pried her mouth open and inserted the small piece of coloured plastic inside her mouth and then simply pulled the bag back loosely to cover her face.

Having completed the task, he considered his work. He knew deep down that she was not his mother but the satisfaction he felt from killing her symbolically over and over again made his whole being feel free and strangely whole.

Peter also realized that there would come a point when he would need to end this and let go of the feeling of pleasure it involved since he only had six of the small plastic Christmas ornaments. Without any more of those he would revert back to, Peter Cassidy, a simple ambulance driver turning sixty years of age. Without the ornaments he could not be Christmas Boy and he would again have to let his mother win.

But that was a few more weeks or months away as he still had three more chances to get his revenge.

Peter collected his pipe wrench and knapsack before he exited the storage building leaving behind all the other items he had brought. He changed out of his scuba suit in the back of his van and rolled it up putting it inside a plastic bag.

Redressed in his street clothes, toque and long coat he drove away knowing that he had left no forensics evidence for the police to find on Monday morning after he notified Detective Ed Morgan of the location of his most recent act of repaying his mother.

Sunday morning Peter was up and dressed and went into the city for brunch at a local restaurant. He contemplated the lives of the individuals, couples and families as they helped themselves to the buffet and loaded their plates.

At times like this he missed the fact that he had no family and when he died there would be no one to mourn his loss. The thought of turning sixty was starting to weight on his mind but he knew there was no chance of turning back to a different life for him.

After lunch he drove to the small hardware store in St Mary's where he had found the Christmas Ornaments and walked around the store looking at all the items on the shelf. He was not sure why he kept being drawn back to this store since he was aware that the ornaments had been old stock that they had sold off.

He bought a new hammer and nails to take back home as he needed to fix the slats on the barn door that were coming loose with age. They were getting dilapidated just like him he thought. As he paid for the purchase, he chatted briefly with the young man who ran the store. When he had been here in October it had been a gentleman in his late sixties that had served him and he had felt a stronger connection with that man who told him that he was the current owner.

"Wasn't there an older gentleman here when I came a few months ago?" Peter asked.

"That would have been my dad," the young man replied. "My parents own the store and I work here and help out but in late October they go to their cottage in Florida for the winter months. He will be back in March."

"Must make for a lonely Christmas" Peter commented.

"Not really, we close the store completely for the week of Christmas and New Year and my family and I fly down to spend the holidays with them."

"Sounds nice." Peter stated. "Thanks for the hammer and nails."

"Appreciate your business." the young man responded.

By the time he arrived home Peter proceeded to write up his email to be sent to Detective Ed Morgan first thing in the morning. He always sent the emails from a proxy server just before he left for work so that the email would be read after he had arrived and on duty at the ambulance office. Then when the call came in for the ambulance to be dispatched to the address, he would be able to respond to the call.

CHAPTER SIXTEEN

Monday morning January 11th Tom rolled out of bed at seven, shaved, showered and prepared to go into the office. Yesterday after church the family had driven to the location on Colborne street where the new church would be constructed and last evening, he had gone back to the church library for the first meeting of the newly elected building committee to discuss the plan of action.

Tom had agreed to be the committee chair with the responsibility of calling future meetings and tracking progress which suited him better then the alternative when his name was passed around as committee secretary. Tom was not keen on being the one responsible to keep all the meeting minutes and paperwork and fortunately the Congregations volunteer office manager agreed to take on that roll.

The Pastor and Bishop were meeting with the representatives of the Thames Valley School board this morning to finalize the paperwork for the sale.

Tom finished his morning ritual and said goodbye to Ann and the boys before heading into the station.

He retrieved his morning coffee and proceeded to his desk in the Task Force "war" room to review any activity or leads that may have come in over the weekend. There was a small pile of typed notes on his desk and he spent the next twenty minutes reading through each one and sorting them by degree of potential. The pile of those that looked promising he sent to the uniformed officers assigned to the task force to follow up with the reporting individuals.

The less promising notes he gave to the desk officer to follow up by telephone in order to clarify, get additional information or mark as non-applicable.

At eight thirty Ed walked into the Task force and stated that there was another email on his computer from the Christmas Ornament killer.

The electronic technician had Ed sign on to the computer in the task force room and then pulled up the email on the large screen at the front of the room.

"Greetings to Detective Ed Morgan and all those who may be spinning their wheels on my behalf. It was another glorious weekend and I have left you another present. This is the Christmas that just keeps on giving! The young lady can be found in a storage room in the abandoned storage building one block north of Longwood Ave on the outskirts of Talbotville heading west. I am sure you will be able to find it from that description. Till next time. Your Friend and nemesis, The Christmas Ornament Killer."

The task force identified the address of the building in question. They then mobilized by contacting the coroner, criminal investigation team and the ambulance service to respond to the scene. The closest available squad car to the site was dispatched to secure the exterior of the building as Tom and Ed headed out of the station to drive to the scene.

The community of Talbotville was essentially part of the greater London city area and was connected to the city without any noticeable breaks in development. When the detectives arrived at the abandoned storage building the attending uniformed officers had sealed off the area and were maintaining crowd control which was critical as the local news reporters started to arrive on the scene including local station news vans.

The Criminal Investigative team and the coroner both arrived at approximately the same time as the detectives and they proceeded to the rear of the building where they noted the back door was slightly ajar. The CI team took over and checked the area around the entrance and the door for any fingerprints or evidence. The team did locate a set of vehicle tire tracks that were on the edge of the grass where a vehicle had parked on the driveway that accessed the rear of the building. It appeared that the vehicle had turned around from where it was parked and had left the driveway leaving a set of rear tire tread marks in the snow-covered dirt.

Photographs were collected of the tire tread for comparison and when they were complete the CI team moved inside the building ahead of the detectives and coroner.

The body of Samantha Jenkins was located in the storage room and Tom noted that the scene was identical to the other two in all the specific details.

After the corner examined the body, he estimated the time of death to be between midnight and four am Saturday morning. He removed the small plastic Christmas ornament from the victim's mouth and bagged it for the criminal investigation team to process.

"If nothing else the perpetrator is meticulously consistent in his actions and how the scene is staged." Ed remarked.

"It would probably be a good idea to engage a criminal profiler at this point as this has all the earmarks of a serial murderer and not targeted homicides which makes it extremely difficult to determine his victims." Tom responded.

"Not real keen on the value of criminal profilers in my experience but at this point any help is better than what we have." Ed stated.

Tom used his cell phone to contact the deputy chief and put in the request that the department contacted a criminal profiler to be added to the task force and advised the deputy chief of the third victim.

The corner was overseeing the removal of the body with the ambulance attendants as the CI team continued to process the scene and bag the clothes, cords, screw hooks, drop cloth and mistletoe.

Tom observed the two ambulance attendants as they worked to place the body in a body bag for transport. He noted the older gentleman of the two as he remembered seeing him at the last two crime scenes.

Tom commented to him." Your job is as bad as mine regarding having to be at the scene and observe all these horrible sights."

"It comes with the job," Peter responded, as he gazed past Tom at Detective Ed Morgan who was staring at the floor where the body had been. That one still doesn't even see me and considers me part of the furniture Peter reflected to himself. The great Detective Ed Morgan is totally stumped and he is less then ten feet away from the one he is looking for. Peter had the urge to laugh at the thought but was able to contain the desire knowing that would simply draw attention to himself.

The attendants picked up the stretcher and proceed with the body to the waiting ambulance passing by the group of photography flashing reporters and the camera of the news van.

For Peter the realization that he would be seen as part of the news reports that were concentrating on the body in the bag was exhilarating to him and added to the sense of satisfaction that he felt from the taking of revenge on his dead mother.

He helped his partner load the stretcher in the ambulance and drove off to the city hospital where the corner would be performing the autopsy. It was unfortunate he thought that he could not be there to witness the autopsy as he would have liked to see her dissected, catalogued and prepared for burial as a final climax to his pleasure.

Tom and Ed watched as the criminal investigation team went through the room and the building in the hope of finding some evidence that the killer may have unintentionally left behind.

When they were finalizing the completion of their work Ed and Tom left the building to return to the station where they were confronted by a group of shouting reporters.

"Can you provide any information on what happened her? Is it another victim of the Christmas Ornament Serial Killer?"

Tom noted that the story had now grown with the addition of the term serial to the Christmas ornament killer. He didn't disagree with the reporters but he knew that adding that to the killer's title would increase the level of fear and panic in the public.

He realized that may not be a bad thing since the killer's pattern was to abduct young women coming out of bars and walking alone at night so maybe the public would get the connection and stop leaving themselves wide open to be targets as the killers next victim.

"We are not at liberty to discuss the details at this time," Ed stated "But it appears that this homicide may be linked to the previous two homicides that have occurred possibly by the same individual. The station public media officer will be releasing information as it becomes available."

Tom noted the arrival of another patrol car and the deputy chief emerged motioning him and Ed over to the vehicle.

"Gentlemen, the mayor and the Chief have been at me since they were notified about the third victim. They want me to come to the scene and make a statement to the press so that we can try to put a positive spin on how 'close' we are to catching the perpetrator.

I know that this is basically public relations window dressing but can you give me anything that can be released to the public to try and align their fears?"

"The best option would be to inform the public regarding the pattern of the abductions and murders. That they involved women in their mid twenties who have been out at clubs or bars and left late at night walking on foot. Advise everyone to stay together in groups and do not be walking alone. In addition, it would be worthwhile to release the fact that the investigating officers located new evidence at the current scene and the task force has been expanded to include a criminal profiler. These could have a positive effect on the public." Tom replied.

"Thanks," the deputy chief stated, "Its time for me to go into the lion's den and get eaten alive."

They watched as the deputy chief walked over to the group of reporters and as he arrived the news van camera lights flashed on bright to illuminate him.

"I would like to start out by stating that we are not releasing the name of the current victim until we have had a chance to notify her next of kin. I can confirm that this homicide is believed to be by the same perpetrator as the two earlier killings attributed to what the media has referred to as the Christmas Ornament Killer. The detectives in charge have advised that we were able to retrieve new evidence at the scene of this homicide which may well assist us in identifying the killer. In addition, the department has requested the Ontario provincial Police provide us with the assistance of a Criminal Profiler to work as part of the task force in order to get a better understanding of the personality and mental state of the perpetrator. "

"Deputy chief, can you provide any advice or suggestions to the public in regard to the serial killer?"

"My best advise is that the perpetrator has shown a pattern of selecting his victims apparently at random from women in their mid twenties who have been walking alone late at night after exiting local bars or clubs. That being the case the advice is for everyone to stay in groups and not be out walking alone at night in order to ensure they do not become a target."

"Is this advice not simply enhancing the fear in the public and virtually turning the people of the city into prisoners? "

"I do not believe we are prisoners but we need to add caution to our activities so everyone can be safe until the police have the opportunity to take this individual off the streets. That is all we have for know but the department will keep you updated as things develop."

The deputy chief left the reporters and headed back to his cruiser so Tom and Ed proceeded to enter their car and left the scene.

"What additional evidence did we get at this crime scene?" Tom queried.

"The tire tracks," Ed snorted back, "May not be anything but at least it gave the deputy chief what he wanted to make the mayor feel better."

The next logical step in the investigation was to inform the next of Kin of Samantha Jenkins and look for any information that might link the three victims to see if there are any connection that could lead to a suspect in the killings.

The background information they received identified Samantha Jenkins as twenty-four years of age. Her parents were deceased and she was listed as residing in the home of her older brother Joseph Jenkins on Colborne street in downtown London.

It struck Tom that the address was just a couple of blocks from the site of the new church where the church building committee planned to build.

It was a neighbourhood that was not far from the downtown and the bar where Samantha was abducted so the assumption was reasonable that this victim was likely walking home after being at a bar the same as the former two.

Tom and Ed knocked on the front door of the home and a lady in her late twenties answered.

"Hello, my name is Detective Ed Morgan and this is my associate Detective Tom Grant. Could you verify if Samantha Jenkins resides at this location?"

"Yes, Samantha is my husband's sister but she is not at home. She went out last Friday evening and hasn't returned home over the weekend. It has happened before that Samantha sometimes stays over at a friends place."

"Might we have a word with you and your husband?"

Mrs. Jenkins invited the detectives to come in and asked them to have a seat in the living room.

She explained that her husband Joseph was asleep as he worked the night shift as a security guard at the local hospital but she would wake him if they needed to talk with him.

"I am sorry for the inconvenience but we really need to speak with both of you." Explained Ed.

Mrs. Jenkins left the detectives and went upstairs to get her husband. She returned and told the detectives that Joseph would be down directly after he got dressed. Shortly thereafter a man in his late twenties appeared in the living room looking visibly sleepy but also showing alarm.

"Is something wrong?" he asked.

"We need to talk with you in regard to your sister Samantha Jenkins, I believe she resides at this residence."

"Yes, Samantha moved in with us when she was seventeen after our parents were killed in a motor vehicle accident on the 401 highway. Their deaths were hard on Samantha. She did not come home over the weekend has something happened." He replied.

"Can you tell us where she was going last Friday evening and who she was planning to be with?" asked Tom.

"She was going out drinking. We have been trying to get her to slow down on the alcohol since it has been a growing concern lately. She has been getting more and more depressed over the last two years. It has become common for her to go out and end up not coming home for several days when she gets drinking with her friends."

"I really need to know, has something happened to Samantha or has she been arrested for doing something after getting drunk?" Joseph asked.

Tom and Ed looked at each other and then Ed responded. "Mr. and Mrs. Jenkins, I regret to inform you that your sister, Samantha, was found deceased this morning. It appears that she died early Saturday morning. Please accept our condolences."

Joseph and his wife looked at each other in obvious shock.

"How did it happen?"

"The indications are that Samantha is a victim of a homicide and we really apologize for the timing but we need to ask you some questions regarding Samantha's activities and plans for last Friday." Tom responded.

"Can you tell us what her plans were Friday evening, who her friends are that she may have been with?"

"Sam has not been very forthcoming with her drinking friends and plans, she has been quiet and slightly stand offish for the past several months, she didn't tell us where she was going just that she was going out to have some entertainment." Mrs. Jenkins replied.

"I have tried to get her to stop the drinking and bar hopping but she wasn't willing to listen. Her only friends we know are Sadie Albert who she has been friends with since high school and her ex boyfriend John Adams. They broke up back in the summer when John said he could not put up with her drinking and partying. I can give you their addresses."

Joseph left to go into the Kitchen and returned with an address book. He copied out the addresses for the two friends he had mentioned and handed it to Tom.

"How was she killed?" Joseph requested and the pain was showing clearly on his face.

"It appears that she was a likely victim of the current serial killer that has been in the news in London area." Ed stated.

"Oh my God," Joseph blurted. "I told her no matter where she was going she needed to make sure she was not on the streets alone after everything I have read. Why wouldn't she listen and simply make sure to be with friends. She usually goes to a bar downtown. I can give you the name."

"Again, please accept our condolences on your loss. You can contact the coroner's office at this number and make arrangements regarding your sisters' body. We will also need you to come to the hospital morgue and verify the identity of the deceased. We can have a patrol officer come and take you if you would like." Ed stated.

Through tears Joseph took the coroners contact card and stated that he would be alright going to the hospital and would not need a police ride.

"You need to get this madman, how can you let him keep killing young women at will like this." exclaimed Mrs. Jenkins.

"We are doing our best, hopefully we will receive a break that will help us find and put away the perpetrator before he can harm anyone else." Ed replied.

Tom and Ed left the Jenkins home and headed to the station to contact the names of the friends of Samantha that they had been provided.

Sadie Albert lived in the east end of the city and they left a message on her answering machine identifying themselves and asking her to call the police station and ask for Ed Morgan or Tom Logan. They explained they simply needed to talk with her regarding any information that she may be able to provide regarding Miss Samantha Jenkins.

John Adams answering machine message indicated he was travelling on business and would be home the following Wednesday evening. The detective again left a voice message identifying themselves and asking Mr. Adams to call the station and ask for detectives Ed Morgan or Tom Grant. They explained that they simply needed to contact him regarding information on Ms. Samantha Jenkins.

Tom considered the realization that by the time they received the voice messages on their answering machines and got back to the detectives it was likely the identity of Samantha Jenkins as the victim in the serial killer homicides would probably have been released to the press.

After lunch they drove to the bar where Samantha's brother mentioned she might had spent the evening in question.

The bar wait staff did remember Samantha. They said that she had been drinking heavily and they had cut her off around midnight shortly after which she had left.

They could not remember her being with anyone in particular and said she tended to shift between tables and groups throughout the bar room, talking and laughing. When she left the waiter remembered that she left alone approximately ten minutes after another group of three gentlemen left.

Tom asked if the bar had any surveillance cameras and the owner replied they had camera's inside the bar in case of disturbances and one outside the bar that filmed the entrance. The staff provided copies of the tapes for the evening in question after which Ed thanked them and they left the establishment.

At the station the security tapes were reviewed. Samantha Jenkins was observed in the bar during the evening and it was obvious she was drinking heavily. There was no indication of anyone who was noticeably paying attention to her during the evening or watching her.

As indicated by the wait staff she was seen engaging with various table groups but was not with any one person. Just before midnight the tape showed three men leaving the bar together and they proceed to walk away from the bar heading up the street.

At midnight the wait staff was observed having a discussion with Samantha which resulted in her responding in an agitated manner corresponding with the account that the bar staff had cut off serving her alcohol. She was then observed coming out of the door of the bar and staggering slightly before she proceeded to walk away down the street from the bar heading in the same direction as the three men who had left approximately ten minutes earlier.

A still shot of the three men as they came out of the bar was captured from the video showing the three men's faces. The detectives hoped this would help identify the men so that the police could locate those individuals for further questioning.

Under normal circumstances the police would simply release the photo and ask if the individuals or anyone who knows the individuals would contact the station as they were potential witnesses that the police would like to question regarding the night in question.

In this case the detectives and the media department both concluded that due to the sensitivity of the case that releasing the photos of the three as persons of interest that they would like to talk to could result in innocent persons becoming the target of the publics growing fear. The public may jump to conclusions that were not intended. The police would therefore have to try and identify the men by talking to the bar staff and other patrons that were they're that evening. Tom and Ed went back to the bar to canvass the bar owner and wait staff regarding the identity of the three men.

Staff recognized the individuals and stated they were frequent customers but could only identify them by their first names. The bar owner remembered that the three had run a tab during the evening for their drinks and one of them had paid at the end of the night with a Visa credit card.

Tom asked the owner if he could provide the name off the card receipt and the owner went into his office returning with the paper receipt copy.

The card belonged to an Alexander Carpenter which the waiter remembered his friends referring to as Alex.

Tom copied the name of the individual and the identification numbers off the receipt.

When they left the bar, Tom called the station and asked them to follow up on the name Alexander Carpenter and provide an address and contact information.

The coroner called later that afternoon and confirmed that Joseph Jenkins had been to the morgue and positively identified his sisters' body.

Tom was informed that the media department was holding a press conference that afternoon at which time they would be releasing the identity of the third victim of the Christmas Ornament Killer in time for the evening news cycle.

That evening Tom watched the six o'clock news report on the homicide and noted that the news was highlighting in red "breaking News" the fact that the Christmas Ornament Killer was now officially listed as a serial murderer. He wondered who the press considered to be the official source that made that statement since the department was not even officially calling the perpetrator the Christmas Ornament Killer. It had been the press who had tagged the killer with that name.

The news report identified the victim as Samantha Jenkins, mid twenties and a resident of London as the reporter talked over the images of the stretcher emerging from the crime scene buildings door and being loaded into the ambulance. The body was covered so that the victim was not seen but the image with the police crime scene tape and officers was a chilling reminder that they had a deranged individual on the loose in their city.

The images were followed by the media interview that was conducted by the deputy chief confirming that Miss Jenkins was likely the third victim attributed to the same murderer.

The police statement then followed with the news anchor talking to "experts" that they had contacted regarding background on serial murders who talked for the next ten minutes about the psychology of multiple murders and the difficulty in catching those individuals.

The news concluded with the call for the police and city officials to "enhance their efforts" and get this perpetrator off the streets of London so the citizens could walk the streets without being in fear of their lives.

Tom understood the fear and hysteria that was growing in London but wondered why the news did not highlight the facts that would allow those being targeted to protect themselves, women in their twenties need to ensure they do not go out walking the streets at night since the evidence identified them as potential targets based on the killers pattern.

On Tuesday morning Professor Brad Collins arrived at the station task force war room and introduced himself as the criminal profiler that the OPP had asked to assist on the case.

Brad was a professor of psychology at a local university and had assisted the OPP with cases in the past couple of years that involved what was labelled as serial killers.

Tom considered what he had read about the relatively newly accepted practice of criminal profiling which entailed the application of the science to assist the police methods for identifying suspects.

In looking up the background yesterday afternoon tom had learned that criminal profiling for serial criminals was being done for repetitive crimes of a sexual and/or homicidal nature.

One case he had read about involved a perpetrator named Clifford Olsen and involved crimes occurring between 1957 and 1981 during which Mr. Olsen had been arrested for offences ranging from armed robbery to sexual assault. In British Columbia there had been a number of children and teenagers murdered between November 1980 and August 1981. Olsen was arrested as a suspect regarding a case of child molestation. He was released due to lack of evidence and continued to murder children until he was arrested and conviction on eleven counts of murder and sentenced to eleven concurrent life sentences. Olsen confessed to the murders under an agreement with the prosecutors that his wife, whom he had recently married would receive $10,000 for each murder he admitted to and then showed police the locations of the missing children's' remains. His wife received $100,000 as Olsen gave the police the location of the first remains of the eleven as a "freebie".

The professional investigative services interest in criminal profiling had started as the result of James A. Brussels profile of the New York "Mad Bomber" in 1956. His profile generated considerable interest in the public when he correctly predicted that the Bomber would be a heavy, single, middle-aged man who would be wearing a double-breasted, neatly buttoned up suit when he was arrested. The practice and science had grown since then and in 1972 the Federal Bureau of Investigations (FBI) Behavioral Science Unit (BSU) in the United States was officially inaugurated following the number of cases of serial and mass homicides that occurred in the 1960's including the Boston Strangler Richard Speck.

The collection of empirical data regarding serial offenders had been collected and recently released with the information from one hundred and fifty nine serial murders (international) from 1795 to 1988 revealing that the most common method used during the process of inflicting death was mutilation (55% of the incidents) (Myers, Reccoppa, Burtoin and McElroy, 1993) . followed by strangulation or suffocation (33% of incidents) and bludgeoning (25%).

The report indicated that serial killers seemed to prefer a "hands on" method to commit a homicide and provides the means to compare the psychological characteristics of serial offenders.[1]

In considering the listing of identified serial killers Tom was amazed by the number and the sheer numbers of victims. Some of those discussed included:

- Aileen Wuornos, murdered seven men in Florida between 1989 and 1990 by shooting them at point blank range. She claimed the men had either raped her or attempted to rape her while she was working as a prostitute.
- Alfred Leonard Cline, known as "Buttermilk Bluebeard," convicted of killing 9 and suspected in two others from 1930 to 1945.
- Alton Coleman, 1984 murdered one man, three woman and three young girls between may and July on a crime spree across six states.
- Andrew Kokoraleis, member of a satanic cult and organized crime group "ripper crew" or "Chicago Rippers" convicted of killing eighteen people over 1981-1982.
- Angelo Anthony Buono Jr who together with his cousin Kenneth Bianchi were known as the "Hillside Stranglers". Convicted of killing ten young women in Los Angeles between October 1977 and February 1978.
- Anthony Edward Sowell, known as the "Cleveland Strangler" arrested October 2009 after the bodies of eleven women were discovered by police investigators at his Cleveland Ohio duplex.

The alphabetized list went on for several pages and left Tom with a sickening felling in his stomach as he realized that the current killer, they were

---

1   Historical foundations and current applications of criminal profiling in violent crime investigations.   Mike Woodward and Stephen Porter.

pursuing would continue to murder young women unless they could catch the perpetrator.

Tom was intrigued with the possibilities that might arise from the use of a professional profiler and planned to work closely with Professor Brad Collins.

Ed on the other hand had made the statement that he didn't buy into this psychological garbage but he told Tom to feel free to be best buddies with the professor and hopefully they could prove him wrong.

At this point Ed was open to any assistance that they could get after the three gruesome murders that had occurred over the past thirty-six days.

Tom sat down with Brad Collins and proceeded to go through the crime scene accounts and evidence reports from the homicides.

Brad studied the photographs of the victims and asked questions regarding the positioning of the bodies.

"In looking at the patterns for the three homicides lets catalogue what we know and the similarity aspects. Where were the victims targeted for abduction?'

"All three were abducted walking on the streets away from local bars or clubs in the London and St Thomas business sections. The times the crimes occurred were estimated between eleven p.m. and two a.m. We canvassed the first two bars during our investigation and were not able to identify any suspicious individuals observed inside or outside the bars regarding the movements of the victims.

We have interviewed family and friends of the victims which did not result in the identification of persons of interest such as past romantic partners, workplace or family disputes, etc.

We have found nothing that links the victims together or where their paths would have crossed outside of being them being selected as victims in the homicides."

"What day of the week did the homicides occur?"

"The victims are being abducted on Friday evenings and murdered over the course of that night at the abandoned locations." Tom commented.

"So, one of the key elements is that the perpetrator is selecting what appears to be random young women in their twenties as they exit bars on Friday evenings." Brad mused.

"Therefore, the key elements for the killer are that the trigger is linked to something that happened on a Friday evening that involved either his mother, family member or girlfriend at some point in his past and involved alcohol.

The staging of the crime scene regarding the bodies is significant regarding the fact he is staking them naked on the floor with their arms and legs secured so they are unable to move but he is not sexually assaulting them."

Brad reviewed the photos of the Christmas ornament and mistletoe.

"This indicates that the incident in the perpetrators past was linked to Christmas and involved mistletoe and this specific type of Christmas ornament.

Based on this my profile would lean towards a male perpetrator who was the victim of an assault most likely occurring when he was a child or youth and unable to defend himself which leads to the likelihood the perpetrator was a victim assaulted by a family member."

"Does this provide any indication of the age of the suspect?" Tom questioned.

"Considering the fact that the Christmas Ornaments you have processed are vintage in nature and have not been readily available in stores for over thirty year I would place his age in the early to late fifties.

Since the homicides have not started till this past month my belief is that the perpetrator has been able to suppress his desire throughout his life since there have not been any similar homicides in the records. He likely has acquired a number of these Christmas ornaments within the past few months which may have been the has trigger for the wave of homicides. The crimes are potentially the acting out related to what ever happened to him.

Based on the time frame the ornaments only recently became available and the fact that the perpetrator is choosing women in their mid twenties the original assault was likely involved his mother or a close female relative when he was a youth.

I will refine my profile but broadly speaking you are looking for a male, mid to late fifties, single, and a professional by trade since he has been able to supress his feelings for a number of years. It is unlikely that he lives in an area that is farther away then fifty miles from downtown London due to his choice of bars and locations where he takes his victims. His job will be one that allows him to travel across the greater London area which would give him the ability to choose abandoned buildings to act out his fantasy.

He is smart with above average intelligence and his emails to Detective Ed Morgan suggests that he has interacted with the detective in the past in some form whether socially or professionally. In fact, the tone would indicate that he holds a deep seated grudge against the detective due to some actual or perceived insult that he received from Detective Morgan."

"So, our best lead is to try and narrow down individuals that Ed has arrested and possibly incarcerated. Possibly someone who has been in a criminal institution for several years and recently released?" Tom asked.

"Not likely that he is connected that way to the detective. The trigger here has been the Christmas ornaments coupled with the detailed repetitive staging pattern of the crime scene plus the fact that the perpetrator is using protective clothing and gloves. This indicates someone who is performing these homicides to satisfy a deep psychological need within the individual and the fact that detective Morgan is the target of the emails is more likely a coincidence due to them having interacted briefly at some point.

This would lead me to believe the individual is in a professional capacity at work that interacts with the police department such as a reporter, city employee, etc."

Tom considered everything that Brad had said but felt they were no closer to finding the perpetrator unless they could find some new evidence to lead them in the right direction and narrow down the suspect pool which at this point was massive in nature.

"I look forward to reading your detailed profile report and working with you closely on this case." Tom commented.

Tom and Brad shook hands and Tom went back to his desk.

The crime scene investigation reports from the third crime scene had arrived on his computer which Tom took the time to review.

The coroners report listed the same information regarding suffocation as the cause of death, the deep gashes including the 'Merry Xmas' on the victim's abdomen had been inflicted prior to her death. The only major different between this autopsy and the first two was the level of alcohol within the deceased system.

The first two had only a small amount of alcohol that was below the legal limit but the third victim had a blood alcohol level that exceeded the legal limit and indicated that she would have been relatively intoxicated when the abduction occurred.

The Criminal investigation report listed the same items found at the scene, victims clothing were neatly piled on a chair in the room, the victim was tied down using the same cord and four turn screw hooks as the prior cases, a plastic sprig of mistletoe was suspended over the victims head and the Christmas Ornament located in the victims mouth was of the same vintage age and design as the other two.

The plastic drop cloth was the same type as previously used.

No fingerprints or DNA was located at the scene other then the victims.

The gauze pad found at the scene contained the same ether like material that was used to incapacitate the other victims.

The tire print located outside the building was matched to the tires that were factory installed on the Dodge Caravan model which was first introduced to the market in 1983 with the 1984 model year. This provided a window between 1983 and 1989 when those particular tires were standard on the Dodge Caravan.

Tom decided to get more detailed information on the Dodge Caravan so he went on his computer and did some research. The Dodge Caravan was considered a revolutionary new vehicle design that was developed and designed by Chrysler Corporation as a smaller alternative to the current Vans on the market and was referred to as a "mini Van". Chrysler was nearly bankrupt and had received a one and a half billion-dollar loan from the United States government.

The company was under the leadership of Lee Iacocca and Hal Sperlich both of whom had been fired by the Ford motor company partially for their insistence and constant push for Ford to develop a smaller version of Ford's popular Econoline, named for minimum exterior, maximum interior design.

The new design needed to meet three critical criteria elements.: the floor had to be kept low enough for women to comfortably drive it, it must be small enough to fit in a standard garage, and the engine had to be far enough from the driver to provide "crush space" in the event of an accident.[2]

Tom realized the information provided nothing definitive but the tires at least give us a potential lead towards identifying the vehicle assuming the tire prints were from the perpetrator's vehicle. Unfortunately, there was no way of determining if the Van had been driven into the driveway by the perpetrator or after the time the perpetrator left and when the investigative team arrived over two days later.

---

2   https://www.smithsonianmag.com/arts-culture/the-minivan-turns-30-9706409/

CHAPTER SEVENTEEN

Tom printed the investigation reports and headed into Eds office to discuss.

"If nothing else this bastard is consistent," Ed snarled as he reviewed the reports.

"He leaves us nothing to go on except the pattern of the killings happening on Friday evening or early Saturday morning. Same method of mutilation and murder. Same set up of the crime scene staging. Same sending of the email notification specifically to me on the Monday morning to identify his crime.

The only additional thing we have is the identification of the vehicle tire tracks but even that is not conclusive in order to lead us to this perpetrator and could have been from anyone who drove into the alleyway over the weekend since the weekend was clear weather-wise and no snowfall after Friday evening."

Tom brought up the criminal profiler's report which Ed waved off as assumption and at best a description that could fit anyone.

Tom discussed the fact that the profile could be useful in narrowing down the pool of suspects with potential age, psychological make up and the fact that the perpetrator had some connection to Ed.

"Okay Rookie, you go ahead and run with this profile if you want to. I am not opposed to anything that may help but I would not hold my breath that it will be of much value." Ed responded. "Our only real lead at this point is to interview this Alex Carpenter and hope that the three of them saw something or better yet are involved and will give us a break in the case."

The name of Alexander Carpenter had been run through the system by records and they had provided a contact address and phone number in London. Tom remembered the photos of the three young men and the profilers report and doubted that they were involved as they simply did not fit the profile. He knew Ed was dismissive and skeptical but after talking with Professor Collins and reading the research on profiling he was more willing to accept the potential values of the science involved and the potential value for the description.

In addition, the credit card company where Alex Carpenter had obtained his card was able to provide the place of employment listed on his records from the credit card application and the detectives intended to stop into the distribution warehouse listed and talk with him.

The balance of the morning was dedicated to Tom sitting at his task force desk reviewing and analyzing the mountain of reports generated from the telephone hot line tips and calls that had been received over the past two days with the news story of the third killing.

Most were speculative reports from people who were suspicious of a neighbour or someone they knew whom they suspected the killer might be. Others were individuals who were afraid to go out of their home since they were convinced a stranger was watching them or following them in a suspicious manner. Others had no bearing on the actual case but were angry citizens who wanted to know why the police were being paid to do their job and were obviously too stupid to catch the perpetrator.

Even the Mayor had been on the news this morning assuring the public that he was doing everything possible to ensure the police do their job and take this menace off their streets.

He went on to explain that the Ontario Provincial Police had provided the services of a psychologist who has provided a criminal profile of the killer and that the Chief of Police had assured him that they were closing in on suspects.

Tom knew that was far fetched and basically an outright piece of mis information but he also realized the Mayor was under extreme pressure from the public and press.

Sadie Albert had returned the Detectives call early that morning and arranged to meet the detectives during her lunch break at a coffee shop next to where she worked in a retail store in downtown London. At eleven thirty Tom and Ed left the station to drive to the coffee shop and meet Sadie Albert.

Sadie was in her early thirties with blond hair and blue eyes. Tom noticed because her blue eyes were such a deep blue that they made her stand out when you looked at her face.

Ed introduced himself and Tom as detectives and told Sadie they just needed to ask her some questions regarding Samantha Jenkins.

"Not sure how I can help, it's horrible what happened to Sam. I have been reading the information in the news and just can't believe it."

"when was the last time you talked to Ms. Jenkins?" Tom asked.

"We haven't talked much in the past year. Before that my boyfriend and I use to get together occasionally with Samantha and her boy friend John to go out to a restaurant or hang out as couples. Sam started to change and to drink heavier, she would show up plastered. I have known Sam since we were teenagers in high school. She was friendly but reserved. She went through a bad spell after her parents were killed and she moved in with her brother and his wife.

She seemed to work through it and was fine till last year when her personality started to change. She just wasn't the same Sam I had known. She started going out to bars on her own and I heard she was having arguments with her brother about the amount of drinking she was doing at home.

I know that it was causing a real issue between her and John. I was with them one evening when Sam was drinking heavy and John asked her to go for professional help. She got belligerent and told John to mind his own business and quit being such a party downer. It was not long after that when Sam and John broke up last summer. Since then Sam just distanced herself from all of us. I really haven't talked to her since then as she told me that I was rude because I wouldn't go out drinking with her. We have just drifted apart."

"Are you aware of any persons in particular that she may have become friends with or that may have had a relationship within the past few weeks?"

"No, as I said we just drifted apart. When I have run into Sam on the street, she generally looks like she has been drinking or is just getting over a drunk. It's sad really as Sam was such a good person and had so much she could contribute. I honestly expected to hear that Sam had died due to her drinking. I understood that Sam was able to keep her job working for a cleaning company that did offices and public buildings but I hear even that was becoming strained with her boss and co workers due to the hang overs ."

Ed thanked Sadie for her information and asked if she thought of anything else that may be important to give his number at the station a call.

After they left Tom and Ed discussed what Sadie had told them and although the information did not provide any clues or pertinent information on Samantha's homicide it did give them pause to consider the tragedy that had become her life.

"You never know what triggers a person to become an alcoholic," Ed commented "But its really too bad. I know alcoholism is a disease not a choice but it can sure ruin a life."

Tom though back to his own family history.

His Grandfather had emigrated to Canada from the United Kingdom in the early nineteen hundreds. He had been a coal miner in Wales all his life before he moved his family to Canada. It was a bit of a misnomer to say he moved his family because he was forced out of the United Kingdom. Tom's grandfather had been a coal miner at the time when the coal miners were disputing with the mine owners over wages and working conditions. The unions were organizing and becoming stronger and his grandfather had been identified as one of the organizers. One morning the police along with a representative of the coal mining company had showed up at the door of their home in Wales and issued a deportation order on the family.

Tom's grandfather, grandmother and children under the age of eighteen were told to pack up their belongings as they were being transported to the seaport that afternoon.

When they arrived by escort at the port the family were given passage on the first ship heading out of the United Kingdom. It didn't matter if it was going to Canada, Australia or another country that was part of the British Empire.

By chance Tom's grandparents, father, aunts and uncles were boarded on a ship to Canada where they had disembarked in Ontario.

The family had settled in the town of Simcoe and the male children got work as weavers in a local factory. Tom's dad had met his mother in Simcoe, got married and lived his life in that town working for the woollen mill.

It had provided a good life and a stable home environment for Tom and his three brothers growing up.

Tom didn't remember much about his grandfather except they lived in an apartment over top of a small shop in downtown Simcoe. His grandfather was an alcoholic and drank heavily eventually going blind and dying from complications of diabetes. What his grandfather did for work Tom never heard and being young he never questioned.

The family were all drinkers at different levels and his dad would often spend the evening getting tipsy.

Tom recalled the night his father had stopped drinking when Tom was in his early teens. His dad had driven over to Brantford to visit family. Brantford was about twenty miles away from Simcoe. His mom and dad had gone out for the evening with the relatives and Tom had stayed at their place with his cousin. When they came back his dad had been drinking heavy but was determined to drive them home at midnight. It was wintertime and the roads were ice covered in spots with 'black ice'.

Tom remembered sitting in the back seat of the car and seeing his father drift over between the lanes of traffic, fortunately the roads were back roads heading to Simcoe and there was very little oncoming traffic. He remembered the accident clearly. As his father came around a bend in the road the roadway was covered in black ice and the car went out of control off the road into the side ditch. There was a telephone pole which the car miraculously missed by scrapping between the pole and guide wire that was stretched from the ground to the top of the pole to keep it upright.

The car ended up against a tree. Tom, his mother and father were all unhurt and the people who lived in the farmhouse came out and helped them inside.

Tom didn't remember how they got home but he remembered the look on his fathers face that evening.

The accident had frightened his dad so badly with what could have happened that he never touched another drink that Tom could recall the rest of his life.

Tom couldn't recall anything being said but the absence of alcohol just seemed to happen.

Tom had started to drink when he was in his teen years and had gotten worse. There was one party when tom had gotten drunk enough that he passed out. In the morning his friends were telling him what he had done the night before as Tom had woken up but he could not remember anything after he first passed out.

That experience along with remembering the reality he grew up with regarding his grandfather and the accident with his dad had caused tom to chose not to take any chances with his family's history of abusing alcohol and decided not to drink. From then on, he would simply not take the chance on drinking.

Tom's thoughts came back to the current case as Ed pulled into the visitors parking in front of the office of the Distribution warehouse where Alex Carpenter was employed.

Ed introduced himself and Tom to the receptionist and asked if they could speak with the manager.

A gentleman in his late fifties came out front and introduced himself as the Operations Manager for the company. He was dressed in a button up shirt and tie with his sleeves rolled up above his elbows.

He invited the detectives to come to his office and offered them coffee or water. Tom and Ed politely refused and then proceeded to explain the reason for their visit.

"We understand that you have an employee by the name of Alex Carpenter working here. We are investigating a homicide and believe that he may be able to help us with some information and we would like to talk to him if that is possible."

"Let me check the work schedule and see if Alex is working this shift and he proceeded to call his foreman out on the shop floor.

It appears that Alex is on shift."

"Would it be possible for us to meet with him privately for a few minutes, we will try to keep it brief and not disrupt your work."

The manager called back to the foreman and after a short discussion stated that Alex was driving forklift but his foreman was arranging for him to come up to the conference room in the front office. He would be here shortly.

The manager then escorted the detectives to a small conference room and asked again if they were sure they would not like a coffee or anything. Ed responded that coffee would be fine and the manager left to have the receptionist bring the coffee.

"Having coffee may diffuse the seriousness of the situation when Alex Carpenter arrives, we don't want the manager to assume that Alex is in trouble with the law and jump to incorrect conclusions."

The manager arrived back with the receptionist and the coffee as a young man in his early thirties arrived at the conference room door.

'This is Alex Carpenter," the manager explained, "Alex these detectives have asked to speak with you."

Ed again introduced himself and Tom as detectives with the London police and that they were investigating a homicide that occurred last Friday evening. They asked if Alex and two of his friends had been at the bar that evening.

Alex responded positively and the detectives explained that he and his friends had left the bar shortly before the subject of their investigation left and the police just need any information regarding what he may have seen along with his companions.

"Joe and Pete were with me, they both work here at the warehouse and we went out for a few drinks. Joe and Pete are co workers here at the warehouse."

Tom asked if they were currently working and Alex responded that they were. Tom asked the manager if it would create too much of an inconvenience if the other two gentlemen could come to the conference room so they could get all three of the statements at the same time.

The manager said that they would be happy to help and went to his office to arrange with the foreman for the other two to be freed up.

The receptionist came back into the conference room with a carafe of coffee and additional cups so Alex poured himself one as they waited. The other two gentleman arrived shortly and the manager left the detectives to talk with the three of them.

Ed again introduced himself and Tom and explained that they were investigating a homicide of a young lady who was at the same bar as the three were last Friday evening.

He explained that the bars surveillance showed the three of them leaving the bar and walking down the street approximately ten minutes before the victim left and went the same direction.

The three of them verified that they had seen Samantha in the bar and that she had been easy to spot because of her actions.

"She was drinking heavy and kept moving from table to table talking to everyone whether she knew them or not. "

"She had stopped at our table a couple of times," Joe mentioned, "she was loud and kind of obnoxious so we didn't spend any time engaging with her hoping that she would move on."

"What about when you left the bar. Did you notice anyone out on the street or acting suspiciously?" Tom asked.

"No, the street was empty. We had parked Pete's car in the parking lot just past the corner of the next side street." Alex commented.

"I was the designated driver Friday night," Pete added, "I did notice one thing as we were walking."

"What was that?" Ed asked.

"I am a bit of an old car buff and when we crossed past the alleyway entrance that was a couple of blocks from the bar, I noticed an older Dodge Caravan parked just inside the entry to the alleyway. It was snowing but the car was just lightly covered and I could see that it was a nineteen eighty-four Chrysler

Dodge Caravan. That was the first year that Chrysler brought out the Caravan and it looked in mint condition."

"Can you provide any more details regarding the car?"

"It was brown but I didn't bother to look at the licence plate. The windows were clear and I didn't see anyone inside the vehicle or in the area. As I said it was in mint condition and the fact that it was a nineteen eighty-four model caught my attention."

"Did any of you happen to see Samantha Jenkins come out of the bar?"

"Sorry we headed to Pete's car, brushed off the accumulated snow and headed down the street driving away from the bar." Alex replied.

"Thanks for your assistance," Tom stated, "And if any of you happen to remember anything else please give us a call."

The three headed back to work and Tom looked at Ed.

"That car could be connected based on the tire description from the crime scene that the Criminal Investigative unit noted. It may be worthwhile to release the description of the vehicle and see if we get any leads."

The two detectives agreed and proceeded to the reception desk of the warehouse where they thanked the manager for his cooperation and the receptionist for the coffee before heading back to the station.

At the station the detectives discussed the potential lead they had received regarding the description of the vehicle with the task force and everyone agreed to release the description of the Caravan.

Tom took on the task of contacting the media department and preparing the press release which would include a representative picture of the type of vehicle in question.

The media department was able to release the information that afternoon in time to make the six o'clock evening news knowing that the printed news media would have the article and description in the next days newspaper.

At six o'clock that evening Tom watched the news broadcast which opened with the information from the press release.

"The London Police Department Major Crimes division has released the following description of a vehicle of interest in the case of the Christmas Ornament Killer.

The police are requesting that anyone aware of a Brown 1984 Dodge Caravan that was observed parked in the area of the bar where Samantha Jenkins was abducted. The vehicle will be similar in appearance to the vehicle represented here:

Detective Tom Grant has requested that anyone who may have information regarding the location and owner of a 1984 brown Dodge Caravan to please contact the Hot Line number which is showing on the screen.

The London Police wishes to thank anyone who can be of assistance."

The reporter then went on to discuss the three homicides to date that have occurred involving the serial killer and advised everyone to be diligent and keep safe. If you are going out at night make sure you are in groups and that no one wanders off on their own so that you remain safe and do not present a target for the killer.

He then aired an interview statement that had been provided by the Mayor:

"The full resources of the London Police and Detectives department are being utilized to apprehend the perpetrator. The Ontario Provincial Police (OPP) are also engaged in the investigation along with officers from the St Thomas Police Department as part of a joint task force.

The OPP criminal profiler has provided the police department with a detailed profile of the Killer and with all this information and the identification of the potential vehicle it is only a matter of time before the perpetrator is apprehended and brought before the courts to be given the justice that is deserved.

Our thoughts and prayers continue with the family and friends of the three young ladies who have been brutally and senselessly murdered."

Tom reviewed in his mind the detailed criminal profile that Professor Collins had provided.

Ed had again rejected the profile as conjecture and did not feel it would provide any assistance.

Tom opened the Criminal Profile of the Christmas Ornament Serial Killer compiled by Professor Brad Collins.

"Based on the evidence collected, the identical staging of the crime scenes, time of the week that the homicides are occurring and the methodology for victim selection I have created this psychological profile to assist in identification of the perpetrator.

The facts have established that the perpetrator is likely reliving a traumatic event in his past, most likely in childhood.

The staging of the crime scene with the victims being naked and tied spread eagle on the floor suggest that this is related to a similar occurrence to the perpetrator.

The mistletoe, Christmas ornaments and the carving of the words "Merry Xmas" indicates the trauma to the preparator occurred at or around Christmas.

The specificity of the antique Christmas Ornament suggest that the perpetrators current activity has been triggered by the obtaining of these ornaments and are similar to what was utilized in his Trauma.

The fact that the perpetrator is selecting young women in their mid twenties would suggest that the traumatic event that he suffered was at the hands of a young woman. In addition, the choice of these women as they exit bars suggests that the women involved in his past occurrence had been drinking or was a drinker.

I have determined the sex of the perpetrator as male because of the strength required to undertake these murders and the choice of victims.

In addition, the fact that he is sending the emails to Detective Ed Morgan would suggest that he is gainfully employed in a profession that would have created opportunities to interact with the police, in particular Detective Morgan. Based on the tone of the emails he believes that Detective Morgan has, at some point, dismissed, ignored or offended the perpetrator and that would explain why the emails are coming to Detective Morgan,

In researching the Christmas Ornaments the origin is vintage and have not been available on the open market for nearly thirty years.

Based on the age of the ornament and the age of the chosen victims it would indicate that the perpetrator is between the age of fifty and sixty years of age.

In conclusion the perpetrator is likely a male between the age of early fifties to early sixties, a loner, is employed in a professional capacity that has or had interacted with the police in the past."

Tom had read the report through several times and felt it could be helpful when they had suspects to compare it too but the only tangible fact at this point is the statement that the perpetrator works in a professional capacity and had contact with the police, particularly Ed Morgan.

Unfortunately, that encompassed a lot of individuals within the system, news reporters, city employees, various agencies, or simply individuals who have interacted with the police due to filing complaints or answering questions on past investigations.

Ed was a great detective but he was not known for his "tactful" manner when talking to people and his brisk attitude could easily have caused offense.

CHAPTER EIGHTEEN

Tom spent the next two days in the task force war room going through the multitude of calls from individuals who were reporting sightings of various Dodge Caravans.

Tom sorted out the ones that were describing Caravans that were different colours to just the ones that were brown.

Officers were dispatched to interview the callers of those vehicles. Based on the interviews the task force could eliminate identifications that were not viable leads that involved simply sightings of vehicles on the highways.

The ones that could provide a definite location were followed up with visits to the locations from uniformed officers. This had eliminated the majority as they were newer models then the 1984 in question or the owners were able to substantiate their whereabouts on the evenings in question.

The exercise was tying up a large portion of the departments resources and not resulting in any single viable leads.

Peter had watched the new broadcast in his farm home including the picture of the 1984 Caravan that was similar to the one he owned currently covered with a canvass cover cloth and locked in the barn.

The identification of the vehicle did not give him rise for concern because of the facts surrounding his ownership of the vehicle.

Peter had spent his life owning used cars and second-hand furniture.

When he had first seen the advertisements for the newly designed 1984 Dodge Caravan, he had felt a strong desire to buy one and be "one of the first" to own it.

He had telephoned around to a few dealerships in London but none of them had any of the vehicles in stock yet but a dealer near Toronto told him they had a brand-new brown Dodge Caravan that had just come into the lot from the manufacturer.

Peter discussed the price and told the salesperson that he would come to Toronto dealership the next day.

On the Saturday morning Peter boarded the train to Toronto from London and travelled to the city taking a taxi to the dealership.

Peter had sat behind the wheel of the new vehicle, took it for a drive and then sat down in the salespersons office to discuss the price. The salesperson had not been willing to move much on the price and Peter did not bring in a trade so they arrived at a price that was agreeable to them both.

Peter had gone into the bank on the Friday afternoon and withdrawn cash to cover the potential cost the salesperson had listed and when they were finished Peter had enough cash to purchase the vehicle outright.

The dealership stated they would need some time to prepare the vehicle for delivery and Peter stated that he would wait.

Later that afternoon Peter had driven from Toronto in his new vehicle back to his home in the country by the town of Allenford.

He got the vehicle registered and licenced and by accident the vehicle registration had listed his vehicle as a 1984 Dodge Coronet since the Caravan was so new as a vehicle type.

Peter had simply kept paying the registration fee every year and the records had never been corrected which meant the police could not track his vehicle through the Department of Motor Vehicle Registration descriptions.

Peter owned a series of used ford cars throughout his life and his current vehicle was a 1987 Ford Bronco that he used for every day driving and going to work.

The Caravan had only been driven sparingly during the first couple of years he owned it and only on the country roads before he had covered it up to keep it in mint condition as his prize possession.

He had lately driven the vehicle on the three nights in question when he had chosen to teach his deceased mother a lesson by taking revenge on the three young women.

Peter was upset by the fact that the car had been identified and left him having to choose if he wanted to risk being seen in the caravan or if he would change his pattern and use the Bronco.

"It just will not be the same" Peter yelled out loud, "It just isn't fair!"

Peter knew he would need to decide but he felt he could leave it for a few weeks since his next plan was to present Detective Ed Morgan with his next present closer to Valentines Day.

He felt the significance of the Christmas presents and the Valentine Present was worth the wait between taking his revenge.

His mother had hated Valentines day. It was a time when she would get drunk for two or three days till valentine's day had passed. During that time Peter never knew if and when she would come into his room and beat him or 'punish" him for making her life a lonely hell. On one occasion she had scarred his back by inflicting small circular burns from her a lit cigarette.

Peter never complained to anyone at school because he felt that in some warped manner, he deserved the punishment and there were no other family to observe what was being done.

Thursday morning started like the day before for Tom sitting drinking coffee at his task force desk and sifting through the call-in hot line leads that had been received.

The Criminal Investigation team had contacted the department of Motor Vehicles and been provided with a computer search listing of all currently licenced 1984 Dodge Caravans on record in the City of London and the greater surrounding area.

The list had provided fifty-four listed current owners.

The list was compared to the owners that the police officers had already interviewed from the call-in leads that had been eliminated and they were left with a remaining total of twenty-one most of which were in surrounding communities such as St Thomas.

Tom asked the officers to follow up on the six listed in the City of London and then contacted the other police forces to obtain assistance in interviewing the other fifteen in the surrounding jurisdictions.

They discuss what the standard questions to be asked were, details of where the owners and the vehicles were on the three nights in question that the abductions occurred as well as what the owner's current employment entailed.

Tom and Ed had received a call back Thursday morning from John Adams, Samantha Jenkins former boy friend and he had agreed to stop by the police station during his lunch break since he worked in an office building not far from the station.

He said he would be happy to help but he had not had much contact with Samantha since they had broken up that past summer.

John Adams arrived at the station at eleven thirty and asked for Detective Tom Grant.

The desk officer called Tom and Ed before taking John back to conference room beside the task force war room.

Ed introduced himself and Tom to John and thanked him for coming into the station to talk with them.

"It's a tragedy what happened to Samantha," John started, "she was heading down a bad road with the drinking but she still didn't deserve this."

"When was the Last time you saw Samantha Jenkins?" Tom asked

"I haven't really seen her since we broke up last summer. I told her that she either had to get help for the drinking or I couldn't stay in a relationship with her. She called me four or five times over the first couple of months. She had been drinking each time and she would alternate between crying and saying she was sorry and she missed me or she would be angry and belligerent blaming me for being a spoiled brat and breaking her heart.

For the last while I simply stopped answering her calls."

"Did Samantha have any other friends that you may be aware that she stayed in touch with?"

"Not really, most of the friends we had in common gave up on Samantha as well. She could be very abusive when she called and she simply was not willing to listen to any discussion about getting help for her drinking."

"We need to ask, can you verify your whereabouts and actions on the three nights of December third, December seventeenth, and January eight?" Ed stated.

"Let me check my calendar.

I was visiting with friends on the third of December and I can provide their names and contact as we went out to dinner and the theater. I have become close with another lady and we were all together that evening till around one in the morning.

December seventeenth I was at my parents in Brampton and spent the night as we were having a family Christmas get together with the extended family on Saturday the eighteenth.

Last Friday the seventh of January. I flew out on business to Vancouver on the Friday as I had meetings to attend Monday through Wednesday. I took advantage of the weekend to visit Vittoria on Vancouver Island. I have air flight and hotel receipts that will verify."

"We want to thank you for your cooperation," commented Tom, "and if you happen to think of anything else that could be of assistance please call the station and ask for Tom Grant or Ed Morgan."

Tom walked out to the front desk with John and thanked him again.

On Friday, the reports from the interviewing officers for the fifteen vehicles came in and resulted in no viable suspects. Many of the vehicles were being kept as trophy vehicles and not used regularly. The owners were able to verify their whereabouts and where their vehicles were located on the nights in question.

"Well that didn't help us much" Ed commented, "We now have a phantom vehicle as well as a phantom perpetrator."

Tom could see the frustration level in Ed was growing rapidly. Ed had spent days trying to go over in his mind anyone who he could associate with the potential profile even though he continuously and publicly described the profiling as useless supposition.

Ed was understandably feeling a sense of guilt because of the fact that the killer was using him as his means of proclaiming his victims.

It was obvious that Ed was upset with the fact that there was some form of connection between the killer and himself and he was trying desperately to find the source of that connection.

CHAPTER NINETEEN

The last homicide had occurred on Friday the seventh of January and there had been no further incidents for the past five weeks. Tensions were running high every Monday morning waiting for the potential of another email proclaiming a kill.

It was the week before Valentines day which was on Monday February 14th and Professor Collins had provided a second report based on the history stating that the weekend of February 11th would be one of potential prime concern as he felt the holiday may trigger the next urge to act on the part of the murderer.

Having that information did not really provide the police with any concrete action that they could undertake to prevent a potential abduction except to put additional officers out on the street patrolling the neighbourhoods where bars were located.

For Tom it had been a stressful five weeks. The hot line tips had eased off after the first three weeks to a trickle and the police were not coming up with any other methods to try and identify the killer.

The past two weeks routine had been for Tom to come to the task force war room and spend the morning at his desk looking through anything that had been received from the prior day's calls, task force meetings and paperwork.

In the afternoon the police duty officer had started to re assign the detectives to other cases to try and better utilize their resources. The Chief had told the department to do the re deployment quietly. The last thing the Chief wanted was the news media and the mayor getting a hint that the force was not dedicating all available resources to the Christmas Ornament Killer.

During the past week Tom had been assigned to attend the scene of a domestic violence complaint that had come in the afternoon on the Monday of week five.

Ed had fluffed off the request to attend the scene with Tom and said he needed to be here working on the critical cases and not going off to babysit a couple of adults who didn't know how to behave themselves.

Tom cringed at Ed's remark realizing that if that got repeated outside of the detective offices it could be construed as an insensitive statement and a violation of department policy. That would result in the department Human Resources getting involved to ensure that the departments reputation would be kept intact and Ed would be subject to some form of discipline.

It made Tom chuckle internally to think of Ed Morgan being forced to take sensitivity training which would be a real treat for the instructor who would have to come up against Ed.

Tom left the station and drove to a home located in the west end of London. A patrol car was out front of the house with a man sitting in the rear seat accompanied by an officer standing outside the rear car door.

The residence was situated in an older neighbourhood of what appeared to be quiet family homes.

The Christmas lights were still hung on the eves and an inflatable Santa Clause was all folded up on the front lawn devoid of air.

He entered the home and approached the officer inside.

"What have we got". Tom queried.

"It appears the husband and wife got into a disagreement about something to do with Christmas and the wife's family. The dispute resulted in raised voices and the neighbours called the police to report the disturbance. When we arrived, we found the wife had been physically attacked and suffered a bloody nose and signs of bruising.

We took the husband into custody and he is secured in the patrol car. The wife is refusing to allow us to call for medical attention and is saying that she deserved it as the fight was her fault.

We have not proceeded with any additional actions and waited for your arrival."

Tom thanked the officer and then proceeded into the family living room. Sitting in an old armchair was a lady in her late fifties. Tom could see the emerging signs of angry red bruises on her face and arms and the women was holding a bloody handkerchief against her nose.

The Christmas Tree was leaning precariously against the wall in the corner of the room where it had been knocked off its base. Glass ornaments were strewn and broken across the floor.

Tom introduced himself as Detective Grant and asked the women if she required immediate medical attention.

When she stated that she did not want an ambulance tom observed her condition and noted that in addition to the fresh bruises that were beginning to show there were also several older visible black and blue marks on the women's arms, and face.

"What is your name?" Tom asked.

"Mary, Mary Saunders she replied." Looking at the floor with a look that Tom perceived as worry and out right fear.

"Can you tell me what happened here?"

"It was all just a silly misunderstanding. My husband Evan is not a violent man under normal circumstances but I provoked him. I should have known better because he has had a couple of drinks and he can become irritated easily.

I was getting ready to take down the Christmas Tree and I asked him to get the boxes out of the attic. He told me he was resting and would do it some other time. I made the mistake of snipping back that the Christmas tree would end up staying here for the next year just like the outside Christmas lights that he left up for two months last year.

Evan got angry and yelled at me that I was being an old hag and nagging him.

I knew I shouldn't have but I yelled back that he was nothing more then a lazy no-good slob since he got laid off from work the first week of December.

I regretted it as soon as I said it but Evan hit me across the face and told me to shut my mouth. I stumbled into the Christmas tree and the ornaments came off breaking on the floor.

That caused Evan to get really angry and we ended up in a shouting match until he grabbed me and threw me down on the floor. He said that I could pick up the broken pieces of the ornaments with my bare hands.

Then he shouted that if I wasn't careful, he would get rid of me and blame it on the Christmas Ornament Killer so I told him I would call the police and have him locked up.

He grabbed me but then the doorbell rang and the officers stated that they were the police.

Evan snarled at me to keep my mouth shut and wipe the blood off my nose before he answered the door.

The officers looked at the two of us and told Evan that he was being detained in the patrol car until a detective from the major crime unit arrived.

Evan started to yell at the officers and even pushed the one officer which resulted in the officers restraining Evan and putting handcuffs on him before they took him outside.

I don't want to press any charges. As I said it was really my fault. I shouldn't have made Evan angry over the Christmas Tree."

Tom advised the officer to contact the ambulance and advised Mrs. Saunders that he was having her transported to the hospital for a medical examination just for her own safety. He told her it was standard procedure in a domestic violence case which was not totally truthful. Tom wanted to ensure she had no severe injuries and have the medical doctor provide a report regarding the older bruises, etc.

When the ambulance arrived, Tom watched as the attendants assessed her injuries, secured Mrs. Saunders into the stretcher and loaded her into the ambulance.

Tom was unaware of the significance of the look that the one attendant used when observing Tom.

"Well, well, well," Peter thought as he worked on loading the victim into the ambulance. "So the department has eased off their search for me which is a good sign." Peter had every intention of pursuing his fourth victim this Friday evening to prepare another present for Ed Morgan for Valentines Day.

He had been watching a neighbourhood bar in the north end of London in a small residential area. He believed that he would be less obvious and could escape detection if he changed to an area out of the downtown cores. He had even stopped into the bar last week and had a couple of drinks near closing time to observe the clientele and the habits of the patrons.

As peter entered the ambulance driver's door he looked back at Tom and thought to himself "Be seeing you real soon."

Tom proceeded to advise the Patrol officer to secure the Saunders home by locking the doors and then the two officers were to escort Mr. Saunders to the police station where he would meet them in the interview room.

One last item that Tom did before he drove back to the station was to call the director of the women's shelter in London and asked her if she would be able to go to University Hospital and talk with Mrs. Mary Saunders.

He provided a short description of the occurrences this morning and simply stated he felt it may be helpful if she could at least discuss the options that are available to her.

Tom realized that it was not technically the police departments job to get involved in the domestic side of abuse cases only to interview the individuals and press charges but only if the injured party was willing to have the spouse charged with assault.

Other then that it was not something that the justice system could take action to proceed on its own resulting in many abuse victims not proceeding. The victims often felt trapped believing in their own minds that they either deserved the abuse, caused the abuse, or were simply to frightened to do anything to stop the abuse.

Tom remembered the information he had read from the women's abuse prevention group.

'Domestic violence is the result of the misuse of power by one adult in a relationship to control another. This control is established through the use of physical assault, psychological abuse, social abuse, financial abuse or sexual assault.

Economic dependence has been identified as the main reason why women stay in abusive relationships since most women in abusive situations do not feel they have the ability or means to support themselves.

In addition, society norms have left women with the feeling that admitting to abuse brings shame upon themselves being identified as battered women. Many lack the information and alternatives which forces them to suffer in silence within their homes. '

Sadly, as indicated by Mrs. Saunders attitude, was the reality that abused women often feel that the abuse is their fault, that they brought on the attack, and that public admitting of the abuse will only cause the spouse to be angrier and cause further harm because they have revealed family secrets.

Even as a detective in the police force, tasked with the role of investigating domestic abuse cases, Tom realized that his ability to intervene was strictly limited under the law which often made these types of "crimes" frustrating for the investigating officers.

Tom also realized that the attitude that Ed displayed dismissing the case was one of the coping mechanisms that police officers had adapted in order to release the frustration involved in the fact that there was basically nothing they could do.

When Tom arrived back at the station, he proceeded to the interview room to confront Mr. Evan Saunders and introduced himself as Detective Tom Grant.

"Good afternoon Mr. Saunders. I assume you know why you are here as a result of the complaint that was filed with the police relating to your argument and subsequent fight with your spouse. I would like to hear your account of what took place."

"I realize that it might look bad but it is not as bad as it appears. My wife and I were having a quiet afternoon at home and had a slight disagreement that the neighbour obviously misunderstood.

Those people are always sticking their noses into other people's business and I could tell you some real stories about their activities."

"I am really not here to investigate the neighbours but the signs of abuse that were apparent on your wife." Tom cut in.

"There is no abuse, Mary got upset at me about the Christmas tree and wanted me to go to the attic to get the storage boxes. I was engaged in watching a show and I told her I would do it later. She got angry and started shouting at me and when I stood up, I accidently knocked her into the Christmas tree. The Tree tipped over smashing some of the ornaments and when she fell into the tree she ended up with a bloody nose.

I admit I lost my temper and started yelling back but that was all that happened."

"Mr. Saunders, your wife showed fresh wounds on her arms and legs and also has what appears to be apparent bruises that are older in nature."

"She is just clumsy and is always banging into things. She probably hit herself against the couch or the table when she fell and was getting up. As I said she is not very coordinated."

"The wounds looked more like they were inflicted by another person and since you were the only one there, we have to surmise that you assaulted your wife." Tom stated.

"Look I have had enough of this. I know my rights. Has my wife claimed I assaulted her and is she trying to lay charges?" Evan snapped

"No, she has not made any statements in that regards at this point but she has been taken to the hospital for examination. I will ask that you remain here till I have a chance to communicate with the officer who accompanied her to the hospital and we get this sorted out." Tom replied.

"Well you better make it quick as I am not going to sit here all day and by the way since you are forcing me to stay here I want a coffee, black." Evan snarled looking very disgusted.

Tom left the interview room and called the attending officer at the Hospital.

"The doctor has determined that the wounds are not severe or life threatening and has treated Mrs. Saunders and is releasing her. A lady from the women's abuse group has also been in talking to Mrs. Saunders but she left since Mrs. Saunders would not have any conversation with her.

I have interviewed Mrs. Saunders and she is claiming that she caused the argument that had resulted in her "tripping" and falling into the Christmas Tree and that the wounds were the result of her own actions. She claims she is not well coordinated and often runs into the door frames and other objects around the house and that is what has caused the wounds."

"Did you advise her regarding her right to lay charges of assault against her husband?" Tom queried.

"Yes, I did but she flat out refused to implicate her husband and said she was not assaulted and would not press any charges. She stated she simply wants to go home."

"Okay," Tom replied. "Provide Mrs. Saunders with a ride back to her residence and give her my card that I gave you. Advise her that she can call at any time if she is in danger from her husband or changes her mind and wants assistance. Hopefully the director of the women's support group was able to provide Mrs. Saunders with her card."

Tom returned to the interview room where he observed that Mr. Saunders was drinking his coffee and looking sullen.

"Mr. Saunders, your wife apparently collaborates your story and she has stated she is not pressing any assault charges. You are free to leave but I warn you that I will be keeping an eye on you and if I ever hear about you being involved in a physical altercation with your wife, I will take what ever action I have available under the law."

"You don't frighten me. I will also have a discussion with the neighbour and tell them to mind their own business in the future." Evan snapped.

"If you harass your neighbours in any manner, I can assure you that you will be arrested and locked up so I would advise you to be very careful in your future actions. I have no qualms about detaining you in our detention facility and I assure you there are individuals in that place that you will meet who take a much dimmer view of cowards who beat women then the police do."

Evan glared at the detective. "Am I free to go."

"Yes you are, I will walk you to the front desk and I trust I will not see you in my interview room again." Tom stated.

"How am I getting home." Evan remarked.

"The desk attendant will be happy to call you a taxi or the city bus route runs two blocks up the street. You are also free to use the desk phone to contact someone to pick you up."

Tom walked Evan Saunders to the front desk and deposited him with the desk attendant. He was not in any mood to offer any assistance or kindness to Mr. Saunders.

Tom again considered in his mind the frustrations that officers felt regarding domestic abuse calls as it left them feeling basically helpless to take any action in most of the cases.

Tom filed his report on the Saunders investigation with the realization that it was a dead issue and would only be useable in the event that Mr. Saunders attacked his wife again and caused serious or life-threatening injuries.

He thought about Mary Saunders and the reality she is living in. By now she would be sitting at home anticipating the return of her husband, not knowing his mood or what he would do when he walked through the door.

Tom also realized that the experience at the police station may diffuse the situation in the Saunders home for a short period but it was only a matter of time before the abuse would happen again.

He secretly wished that Evan Saunders was hot headed enough to verbally threaten the neighbour or create a nuisance on their property so that Tom could formally charge him and take legal action under that approach.

CHAPTER TWENTY

The week dragged on with Tom and Ed reviewing the small number of leads. As the Valentines day weekend drew near the tension levels became more predominant based on the assessment that the profiler had stated that this weekend would be a prime weekend of concern.

The police force was on alert with the increase of additional patrol officers who would be circumventing the streets in the areas where bars were situated on Friday evening. They had been told to be on the watch for a brown 1984 Dodge Caravan on the streets of London.

Friday February the eleventh arrived with a fresh blanket of snow dusting the roadways.

Peter arrived home from his shift at the ambulance station and proceed to prepare his kit for the evening's activity.

He packed his duffel bag with four screw hooks, cord, plastic drop sheet, mistletoe, pipe wrench and duct tape.

He carefully wrapped the fourth of his six plastic Christmas Ornaments in protective cloth and placed it on the top of the supplies along with his sprig of plastic mistletoe. The final item he placed into the bag was the scalpel, gauze cloth and bottle of liquid that he would use to temporarily anesthetize his victims. In addition to the duffel bag he placed the folded rubber diving suit in the rear of his 1987 Ford Bronco. He softly lamented that it was not right that he couldn't use his Dodge Caravan and had to change his routine but he did not want to take the chance on someone seeing and identifying his treasured vehicle.

He slowly uncovered the 1984 Dodge Caravan and stared at the unblemished vehicle that he loved.

He turned on the engine and listened to the quiet purr before he shut it off and re covered it with the tarp.

Peter then went into the house to shower and make his supper.

At ten p.m. he put on his long coat rechecked his kit and drove away from the farmhouse heading for the designated bar he had chosen for this evening's activities.

Traffic was relatively light as he made his way down Hyde Park Road to Fanshawe Park Road and drove towards the north end of London.

He had selected an abandoned barn on Sunningdale Road just outside of London as his choice for tonight's activity and had driven past it several times over the past few weeks ensuring that the barn was unused both in the daytime and at night.

The feeling of anticipation and revenge against his mother grew within Peter as he recalled the actions of his mother at Christmas and Valentine's Day in his youth. He did not feel any remorse or regret for the young women and only associated them with his drunken mother. They were simply a means for him to get his revenge against the real culprit, the real perpetrator that had made his childhood an unbearable hell and destroyed his life.

He arrived on the street and slowed a block down from the bar well before eleven p.m. proceeding to park his vehicle on the side of the road under a streetlight that was not working to provide some semblance of darkness for his planned work.

At eleven p.m. Peter noticed a patrol car coming down the street and slowing down as it approached the area where he was parked. He slumped down on the front seat out of view of the passing officers. Once they went by he sat up and chuckled to himself. Out looking for a 1984 Dodge Caravan I reckon, not interested in my Bronco.

Just before eleven thirty he noticed a young lady emerge from the bar and walk towards him. He had assumed properly that anyone coming out of the bar would be heading towards the intersection past where he was sitting to catch the municipal bus at the bus stop on the corner of the street.

Peter had disengaged the dash and dome lights inside his car and he quietly slipped out the driver's door in the dark shadow provided by the burnt-out streetlight.

He crouched behind the rear of the bronco with his gauze cloth and as she approached, he sprinkled the liquid from his bottle on the cloth in preparation.

Placing the closed bottle in his pocket it seemed as if time had slowed down as she walked towards his hiding place.

He peered stealthily around the back bumper and noticed that the woman had slowed down and stopped as she was staring at his parked vehicle. He held his breath in anticipation until she finally started to walk again towards his Bronco.

Peters heartbeat seemed to slow along with his breathing as he moved behind the far rear fender of the car while she passed.

It felt like a challenge to him, a game as she kept peering towards the Bronco and looked inside carefully as she passed.

When she was past the back of the vehicle Peter saw her look back towards the bronco before she pulled her hood up over her bright red hair and started walking faster towards the corner.

Quietly, stealthily like an animal stalking its prey Peter came from behind the Bronco and in perfect silence on the new dusting of snow came up behind her and grabbed her around the throat placing the cloth over her nose and mouth.

She took Peter by surprise momentarily by reaching up with her right arm and releasing a spray fully into Peters face over her shoulder.

Peter was enraged and even though he felt the burning pain in his eyes and mouth he tightened his grip on her throat and over her nose and mouth till she slumped backwards into his arms.

The burning was excruciating as peter realized that she had used pepper spray. She must have been carrying it in her hand when he grabbed her and she had reacted quickly. Peter had seen oleoresin of capsicum (pepper spray) used on individuals before that they had treated on ambulance calls. The inflammatory effects cause the eyes to close temporarily blinding the victim.

Peter struggled through his tear-stained eyes to locate the Bronco and load the woman in the back. Normally he would duct tape the victim but his vision was impaired to the point he needed to wash out his eyes with snow before he could do anything else.

Slowly his vision began to return but the pain continued.

He proceeded to duct tape the woman's wrists and ankles. Placing duct tape across her mouth before he got into the drivers' seat and started the engine.

He needed to get away from the scene before anyone else exited the bar or the random police patrols came by. He drove away from the bar heading towards the barn on Sunningdale Road.

Slowly his eyes became clearer and the rage in Peter grew at how this woman had again inflicted pain upon him reminding him of his youth. He vowed that tonight she would pay dearly for this.

When he arrived at the farm, he opened the driveway gate and proceed to drive the bronco inside stopping to close the gate behind him. He drove the bronco inside the empty barn closing the barn doors.

He peered outside to see if there were any visible tracks coming into the barn that could be seen by passing vehicles but with the softly falling snow, he knew that this deserted stretch of road would be an unlikely use for others.

He unloaded his kit from the Bronco putting his clothes neatly in the back seat and donning the full body rubber divers' suit and rubber gloves. He then went to work laying down the plastic tarp.

He felt a surge of excitement as he slowly undressed the unconscious woman and folded her clothes neatly on a barn stool beside the open stall.

He had never been with a woman sexually and had no real desire for intimate contact but the sight of the naked bodies made him tingle as much in anticipation of the evening activity as the rise in hormones. He wondered if this feeling was similar to lust.

That was not to say that he did not feel a form of sexual satisfaction in the act of re paying his mother but that rush would come as he watched the life drain from their face covered by the plastic bag This inevitably resulted in the discharge of semen inside his rubber wet suit. That was why Peter was careful to ensure he was wearing adult incontinence diapers so that no DNA could possibly be discharged and left at the scene.

He took the limb body of his victim inside the stall and laid her on the painter's cloth.

Carefully he measured the lengths of cord he needed to secure both arms and legs by the wrists and ankles. Having measured the distance, he proceeded to drive the screw hooks into the wooden plank floor using the pipe wrench for leverage.

The barn floorboards were old and soft so the task was not as difficult as he had experienced in some of the other locations and within a short period of time the victim was staked out spread eagle on the floor on top of the plastic sheet unable to move with the exception of the fact she could wriggle her body during the 'punishment.'

Harriet Carter awoke from her drug induced sleep to the realization that she had been abducted. She felt the cold air of the barn on her naked body as she lay upon the cold plastic sheet.

In a panic she remembered the feeling of the strong arm coming around her throat and the smell of the gauze cloth that had covered her face. She remembered reaching over her shoulder with the pepper spray she was carrying in her hand but could not remember anything else.

Her mind raced back over the occurrences of the afternoon and evening.

Her fiancée Jeff had decided to go on a hunting trip with his friends instead of spending Valentine's weekend with her. He promised he would be back Sunday night and they would spend Valentines day together but Harriet had been hurt and angry that Jeff would rather be hunting with his friends then with her as they planned their upcoming wedding. When her girl friend Julie called to see what Harriet was up to the invitation to get together for a drink at a neigh-bourhood bar sounded appealing. Harriet did not routinely go out drinking and rarely went to bars especially alone but Julie said she would meet her there by eleven so Harriet decided to go,

She had arrived around ten thirty and ordered a drink as she waited. Around Eleven Julie called and apologized but she said she had gotten tied up in a family emergency and could not make it. Julie had ordered a second drink while she chatted with the bar tender before she left the bar just before eleven thirty.

The bar tender had suggested that she take a taxi but Harriet knew that the bus stop was only a few blocks up the street and decided the walk would clear her head.

It amazed Harriett how quickly everything passed through her mind as she struggled to be freed from the cords that held her.

Out of the corner of her eye she saw the flicker and glow of a cigarette burning in the darkness.

Slowly the burning ember raised up and a man walked into the pale light of the kerosene lamp that was placed beside Harriet's head.

Oddly Harriet felt relieved that her naked body was lying face down on the plastic as it seemed to provide her some comfort that the man was not looking at her naked breasts and pubic area.

"Well, its about time you woke up," Peter stated softly. "That pepper spray really stung and you are going to have to pay for that."

Harriet could not speak through the duct tape covering her mouth as the panic welled up within her.

"have you ever felt the pain of a lit cigarette against your skin." He commented softly.

Slowly he took his cigarette and pressed it against the skin of her buttock sending a stab of burning pain through her body. He methodically applied the cigarette to her upper thighs and back as Harriet writhed in pain from the searing heat and pain. The smell of burning flesh filled the barn.

Peter stopped and went back to his place in the darkened corner of the stall as Harriett's sobbed through the duct tape and tears poured from her eyes.

The burning pain was constant and her whole back felt like it was on fire.

Slowly peter put out the cigarette and lit another which flickered brightly as he drew in the air through the cigarette.

"You know mother that this is all your fault." Peter whispered.

Harriet's mind was too filled with trying to cope with the pain to understand the words that were being said.

Peter rose from the floor and came over to kneel beside her side again and then the fresh pain started again as Harriett felt the new surges of agony from the hot tip of the cigarette on her back.

The waves of pain and the smell of burning flesh resulted in Harriet's mind shutting down and she again went into unconsciousness.

The next time Harriett regained consciousness her mind tried to comprehend that something was different. The searing pain from her back was still rushing through her mind but now she slowly realized that the pain in her back was against the cold plastic cover.

She was lying face up and spread eagle on the floor.

She struggled to comprehend as she saw the shape of her attacker moving towards her only this time instead of a burning cigarette, she saw the glint of a silver blade in his hand.

"Time to proceed to our regular Christmas ritual mother." Peter spoke softly in the darkness.

Harriett moaned through the duct tape covering her mouth with a sound more animal then human in its desperation.

The burning pain in her back was then heightened by the deliberate cuts of the scalpel cutting deep ribbons into the skin of her chest, stomach, arms and legs.

This time it took less time before her mind sank into protective unconsciousness.

For Peter it seemed like an eternity waiting for Harriet to regain consciousness this time and he was afraid that her body may shut down from the pain which would rob him of his final act of watching her die. He had removed the duct tape covering her mouth and would routinely check her vital signs to ensure she had not passed away.

It was nearly three thirty in the morning when Harriett slowly regained a level of consciousness indicated by her pitiful moans so Peter placed the plastic bag over her head.

When her eyes reluctantly flickered open he said." Glad your back. Happy valentines' day and Merry Xmas." He said as he taped the duct tape tightly around the plastic bag at her throat cutting off all air to Harriet's mouth and nose.

Her body reacted in panic as she struggled to draw air into her lungs but only succeeded in sucking the plastic of the bag tightly across her mouth and nose until her body gave up its fight to live.

Peter sat and stared into her eyes as she succumbed to the loss of oxygen and he felt the surge of anticipation and the flood of release that was contained within his swimsuit diaper.

After all life had left the woman on the floor in front of him, he removed the tape from her throat.

Going to his duffel bag he carefully removed the fragile plastic Christmas ornament and placed in inside the victim's mouth replacing the plastic bag loosely over her face.

Now was the time that peter needed to re pack the duffel bag with the remains of the cord, the wrench and any other items. He had brought a glass jar which he had used to hold the extinguished cigarette butts and he sealed it gingerly to ensure that no DNA from the cigarette remains could be found.

After he placed the bag in the back of the Bronco he returned to the body and did one last thorough inspection of the scene until he was satisfied that the great Detective Ed Morgan would have nothing to point him to Peter and he left the area carrying the lantern that had been the source of his light during the three hours of his revenge.

He took off the rubber divers' suit and gloves at the back of the Bronco standing on a plastic drop cloth to ensure nothing was missed. He wrapped the suit and the discarded diaper in a ball and placed them inside a plastic bag he kept for that purpose.

Once he was dressed back into his street clothes and long coat jacket, he again checked the area around the Bronco to ensure nothing remained from his nights activity before he opened the barn door and backed out onto the driveway.

It was nearly five a.m. when he drove through the gate and headed back on the deserted roads to his farmhouse home. He felt the inevitable surge of fatigue that always overcame him after the nights work was completed.

Snow was softly falling covering the tracks of his vehicle that remainded on the driveway and by the time anyone would be driving down this stretch of lonely road there would be no visible sign of Peters entry into the abandoned barn. That was the way he wanted it till he sent his email Monday morning to Detective Morgan which would result in Peter again re visiting the scene. The surge of excitement and adrenaline that overcame Peter each time he got to watch the police and especially Ed Morgan stumble around the sight of his pleasure added to his satisfaction for a task well done.

When he arrived home, he parked the Bronco in the driveway and removed all the paraphernalia from the nights activity and put them into the storage box in the garage. The rubber diver suit he hung over the drain in the empty stall and proceeded to wash down the blood and body fluids into the septic tank drain.

He threw the discarded diaper in the trash barrel behind the barn so he could burn it later that day.

With the ritual completed Peter went into the house, ate breakfast and then went to his bedroom to spend the day sleeping off his tiredness and fatigue.

CHAPTER TWENTY ONE

On Saturday morning Tom and Ann had plans to take the kids spend the afternoon in Simcoe visiting with Tom's brother James and his family. Tom had prepared a surprise for Ann since he would be working next Monday on Valentines day.

James and Gladys had agreed to watch the boys later that afternoon and Tom had made reservations to take Ann to the Erie Beach Hotel in Port Dover for a surprise early dinner.

The Erie Beach Hotel was a landmark in Port Dover and just a short walk from the popular Port Dover beach on the north shore of Lake Erie. The hotel was once a famous summer resort where people could stay for ten to twelve dollars per week including meals.

In nineteen forty-six Harold and Marjorie Schneider purchased the historic hotel and started the tradition that became famous for their home cooked meals.

In the early nineteen seventies their son Tony and his wife took over ownership of the hotel and added more dining options to the facility.

The hotel's Cove Room restaurant was very appealing and Tom and Ann enjoyed the Lake Erie Perch Dinner that came with a variety of salads served on a trolley at your table so that you could help yourself. In particular, the fried celery bread was a well-established favorite at the Erie Beach Hotel.

The evening Tom had proposed they had dinner in the cove room and then went for a walk along the beach board walk where Tom had hesitantly asked Ann the question of whether she would be willing to share the rest of his life.

Ann and her girlfriend, Maggie had been planning for the two of them going to Europe to travel after graduation before Tom met her and Tom was not sure how she would react to his proposal of marriage which would change the plan.

Ann looked at Tom and asked one simple question: "Why?"

Tom's reply had been, "Because I love you and want you to be with me."

Ann had said yes and things had progressed from there.

At ten a.m. the family set out for the ninety-minute drive to Simcoe to gather at James and Gladys home for a light lunch and visit. Ann did not have any inkling of Toms' plans for four o'clock that afternoon.

In his pocket Tom had a small package containing a heart shaped pendant which he had kept hidden in anticipation of this afternoon.

It could be said that Tom was not much of a romantic and is not known for his gestures but today he wanted to show the mother of his sons how much she meant to him.

The afternoon lunch and visit at his brother's place was filled with laughter and family memories allowing Tom too to compartmentalize and set aside the three grizzly murders. Relieving the stress that was tangible in the air in London and at the station.

At Three thirty he asked Ann to go for a ride and Gladys immediately stated.

"Leave the boys with us so they can get to know their cousins better. You two take a break for a little while."

Ann was startled but after some discussion she agreed to leave the boys 'for a short visit' and her and Tom went out to the car.

She looked at Tom suspiciously as they drove out of Simcoe heading towards the town of Port Dover and was even more surprised when Tom stopped and parked in front of the Erie Beach.

"We have dinner reservations." Tom declared "Hope your still hungry."

Ann was pleasantly shocked and took the surprise in stride as they entered and spent the next hour having a casual meal together.

"This is nice." Ann commented, "but why."

"I am working Monday and will not be able to treat you for Valentines Day so I arranged this for today," Tom smiled.

After they had finished their meal Tom suggested a walk along the beach boardwalk in the soft layer of white snow. When they reached the spot where Tom had proposed he took out the small felt covered box and gave it to Ann.

She opened it and her eyes welled up with tears.

"I love it." She proclaimed.

"I love you." Tom replied.

Tom closed the clasp on the chain after Ann placed the pendant around her neck.

They drove back in quiet contentment to James home and after Ann finished sharing the story of their dinner they prepared to pack up the boys and head for home.

"You know you are a real pain in the butt." Tom's brother proclaimed. "How am I going to live up to what you did on Valentines Day for Gladys."

"I guess that's your problem Brother but I have established myself as the romantic one in the family for today."

The brothers laughed and goodbye hugs were shared all around before they drove back to London.

On Sunday morning when the family went to church Ann was wearing her pendant and was proudly sharing the story of the previous day with everyone at church.

After church while everyone else shared in coffee and snacks Tom was enclosed in the church office with the new building committee as they started the task of preparing to review architectural drawings and plans for the new church home.

Once the committee had narrowed down the designs to an overall draft, they would have a congregational meeting so everyone could provide their input and ideas in order to come up with an acceptable layout.

It was estimated that the finalization of the plane would take two to four months since every member of the congregation had to feel involved and have ownership in how the new church building would be designed as their spiritual home.

Following church, the Grant family went to the home of Ann's parents to visit and have lunch where Ann again shared her pleasure at the gesture Tom had done.

Tom knew he had scored points big time this weekend in their relationship and he felt a surge of contentment with his life.

Peter spent the balance of the day Sunday preparing his thoughts for the email he would send first thing Monday morning. The excitement and exhilaration of the weekend was still surging through him and he felt invincible.

He was already beginning to plan his next weekend adventure when he would again satisfy the need to punish his mother. The sight of dead, hurting and pain filled people that he encountered in his work life had for so many years provided him with the ability to suppress the darkness that kept rising up in him.

He was now overcome with the need to lash out and fight back at this point in his life.

On March twenty fifth he would be sixty years old and this birthday felt like a turning point in the course of his life. He felt tired and that he had lived too long. Peter had every intention of ending his life once he had completed the use of the six plastic Christmas Ornaments that had formed in his mind staring him down this road.

These months were like the climax of everything that he had suffered and lived through, the pain, the abuse, the loneliness, the dismal pattern of his existence.

His plan was to complete the fifth weekend to celebrate St Patrick's Day which was scheduled for Thursday, March seventeenth. He would repeat his pattern on the Friday of March eighteenth.

The final time he would use the sixth and last ornament would be Good Friday, April first, Easter weekend.

That would be the climax in which he could belatedly celebrate his birthday and complete his life journey. It felt fitting to him that on the weekend when all the Christian world would be celebrating a sacrifice that he to would be sacrificed.

He had it all planned in his mind, the final Friday activity. The final Monday to see the face of Ed Morgan one last time and then he would send an email to the great Detective Ed Morgan one last time revealing who he is and how he had led the whole department on a fruitless hunt for all these months.

He would write up his final letter to tell the world what he had suffered and why these others had to suffer to repay his mother before he would take a bottle of pain killers that he had removed slowly one by one from the ambulance until he had more then enough for a lethal dosage.

He often imagined in his minds eye the frustrated look on the face of Detective Morgan when he found the dead body of Peter Cassidy knowing that he had not been able to catch him or stop him. That the great Ed Morgan was impotent to identify someone who was close to him at every scene and Peter relished the fact that Morgan would feel defeat that would cause regret for the rest of his career because he never solved the case of the Christmas Ornament Killer.

Peters only regret would be that he would not be alive to see his name rise from anonymity to being known country wide as reporters and professors and lawyers would write papers and have long discussions about the man who killed at will and was never caught by the police.

It was Sunday afternoon after Peter completed his supper that he sat down at his computer and wrote up the email to Detective Ed Morgan to proclaim this weekends present.

CHAPTER TWENTY TWO

Monday morning Tom got up and headed to shower. He past the boys room and peeked in to see that they were both asleep as he went into the washroom to prepare for the day. When he came out to get dressed, he was surprised to find that Ann had got up as well. This was not the normal routine as Ann generally slept in till after eight when the boys would start to rise. Tom walked into the kitchen to the smell of coffee and bacon.

"What's all this?" he queried.

"I just felt like making my husband's breakfast for Valentines day before he headed off to fight crime on the streets of London."

"I could get used to this." Tom replied.

"Well don't because this is a one-time gesture to thank you for a lovely weekend. I will continue this day's celebration by preparing a special supper when you get home from work this evening."

Tom smiled and sat at the kitchen table to eat his breakfast before he headed to the station.

"Are your parents coming over for supper this evening?" he queried.

"Yes they are and after supper mom and dad are going to take the boys to stay overnight at their place. We will have the evening at home alone."

"Sounds intriguing," tom stated, with a twinkle of anticipation in his eyes.

He kissed Ann goodbye and drove off to the station feeling elated.

His mood continued as he entered the war room with his 'second' cup of coffee for the day. As soon as he was seated at his desk and started up his computer Ed Morgan stuck his head in the door of the war room and snarled.

"Get your butt into my office, we have another email."

Tom hurried into Eds office and they stared at the screen of the computer which proclaimed that Ed had an email.

He hadn't opened it before he called Tom to join him.

The subject line sated "Happy Valentines Day from your friendly neighbourhood serial killer."

Tom called the deputy chief who advised them to meet in the war room so they could bring up the email on the main screen to allow the forensic technicians to open it to see if there was any way that they could identify the sender.

In the war room the team gathered around the main screen as the technician brought up Ed's email account and proceeded to try and identify where the email had originated by locating the IP address. The same as before the IP address lead to a public server and had been sent as a ghost account.

The group watched in anticipation as the technician determined that there was no means to identify the sender and opened the email.

"Good morning to the 'great' detective Ed Morgan and all the other flunkies who will undoubtedly be with you.

Valentine's day weekend was an ideal time for me to extend my series of Christmas presents to you and I have chosen a special one for Valentines Day. She has bright red hair, the colour of Christmas and Valentines hearts to tie the two holidays together.

Since you have been so patient in letting me complete my series of presents and haven't interfered in the least by coming close to finding me, I am going to give you a clue in anticipation of my fifth present. Unfortunately, I will not be able to find someone with 'green' hair to tie in that holiday season but it's the gift that counts, not the wrapping.

My gift for valentine's day is located in an abandoned barn on Sunningdale Road past Highbury on the right-hand side. You'll be able to find it as it is approximately three miles from Highbury. Since your detection skills are limited, I will give you some glues, next to the closed metal farm gate there is a clump of tall evergreen tress and a hedge of picker bushes growing up the laneway to the barn.

The Christmas Ornament Killer."

The deputy Chief proceeded to have dispatch advise any patrol cars that may be in the vicinity of the described crime scene to proceed to Sunningdale Road and locate the barn in question. Instructing the, to cordon off the area to prevent any press from entering the scene before the investigating detectives, criminal investigation team and the coroner.

No one held out hope that the victim would be found alive having seen the three prior scenes and the key was to preserve the scene and gather any evidence that the perpetrator had left behind.

Tom and Ed left the station in their vehicle and headed north on Highbury Ave heading to Sunningdale Road.

Sunningdale Road was more of a farm lane then an actual city street. The detectives observed tire tracks along the road that lead them to the stopped patrol cars with flashing lights blocking access to a farm gate that was slightly open.

The attending patrol officer that was the first to arrive had taken charge of the scene. He had only disturbed the scene by having one officer walk carefully up the laneway to verify this was the barn in question.

Tom looked at the lonely set of footprints in the snow going to the barn and coming back.

The officer verified that the barn did indeed contain another body and the officer noted that the body had been there for some time so he returned to the road to wait for the criminal investigation team. As they were talking the criminal investigation team arrived and proceed to process the gate and the laneway methodically up to the barn after which the gate was opened and the detectives and coroner proceeded to walk up the lane way to the old barn that stood before them.

As they entered the barn the criminal investigation team went to work processing the scene which was similar in all aspects to the other three. The body was laying spread eagle and naked on a plastic drop cloth and was staked out by the wrists and ankles in a horse stall.

Her clothes were piled neatly on a wooden stool and the identical piece of plastic mistletoe hung over her head from the beams.

The perpetrator had slashed deep cuts across different parts of her body, arms and legs and had carved the words Merry Xmas into her stomach.

The corner estimated the time of death as sometime overnight between Friday evening and Saturday morning. The fact that the body had been exposed to the freezing cold temperature in the abandoned unheated barn had made a more exact time impossible to estimate.

He removed the plastic bag which the Criminal Investigation team secured as evidence and removed the small plastic Christmas Ornament from the victim's mouth.

"I will not be able to confirm for sure until I do the autopsy but it appears that she has been killed by suffocation the same as the other victims." He stated.

At that moment, the ambulance attendants arrived with a stretcher and body bag at the door of the barn and waited for the coroner's instruction.

Peter watched as the coroner covered the body of Harriet Carter with a white cloth and motioned for the attendants to remove the body to the morgue.

"You haven't even turned over the body to see my extra efforts on this one." He thought to himself.

As the lead attendant Peter had the stretcher situated on the ground next to the body of Harriet so that when they turned the body on its side to place her on the stretcher, he could deftly let the sheet drop exposing the burns on her back.

"Hold up," the coroner stated. "Look at these burn marks. This is new as there were none on the other victims."

Tom and Ed knelt beside the coroner and examined the angry red circles. The coroner stated that the marks were most likely from the woman being burned with a lit cigarette.

"What do you make of this," Ed asked Tom.

"Its certainly a change in pattern from the others." Tom replied

The coroner had the ambulance attendants recover Harriet's body on the stretcher and they proceed to remove her from the scene.

Peter had to restrain himself from laughing out loud as he looked at the puzzled face of Detective Ed Morgan. "Well at least that got your attention." He mused to himself, "Even if I am still invisible to you when I am only ten feet away."

The criminal investigation team had located Harriet's cell phone amongst the pile of clothes and gave that inside an evidence bag to Tom so that he could have the forensics technicians see if they could identify who Harriet had contacted. Her wallet provided her home address as an apartment on Fanshawe Park Road that was in the northern part of the city.

The detectives decided to stop into Harriet's apartment building as thier first stop on the way back to the station.

When they arrived at the apartment building Tom noted that fact that it was a small building containing only six apartments and the address listed number six as Ms. Carter's.

When the detectives knocked on the door it was opened by a young man in his mid twenty's who was dressed in blue jeans and a pullover shirt.

Tom and Ed introduced themselves as London Police Detectives and asked if this was the apartment of Harriet Carter.

The young man responded in the affirmative but stated she was not at home currently.

Ed then asked if they could come inside and have a few words and the young gentleman opened the door inviting them inside.

"Can I ask who you are and what your connection is to Ms. Carter." Tom asked.

"My name is Jeff Coles, Harriet and I are engaged to be married in just under two months. Can I ask what this is all about? Has Harriet been in some sort of accident?" Jeff responded and Tom could sense the tension and panic growing in his voice.

"When was the last time you saw Harriet?" He questioned.

"Friday morning. I went on a hunting trip for the weekend up north with two of my fiends. Sort of a bachelors last fling since Harriet doesn't care much for hunting. We made it a long weekend taking Friday and today off work and got back about nine this morning. Harriett isn't home so I assume she has gone to work." Jeff stated.

"Can you provide us the names and contact for your friends that you spent the weekend with." Ed asked.

Jeff provided the names and phone numbers but Tom could see the apprehension welling up in him and being demonstrated in his body language.

"Mr. Coles," Tom started "We regret to inform you that Harriet Carters body was found this morning indicating that she has been deceased since sometime Friday evening or Saturday morning."

"What." Jeff responded with a look of bewilderment. "That can't be possible. I had plans with Harriett to spend this evening making up to her for my hunting weekend with a surprise for Valentines day. How did this happen?"

"She appears to be the victim of the serial killer that has been identified as the Christmas Ornament Killer by the press." Ed stated. "We will need you to come to the morgue and assist us by identifying the body."

Jeff shook his head yes but his whole countenance was masked in disbelief and the shock of the realization of what he had just been told.

"Can you provide us with the names and contact information for Ms. Carters family?" Tom asked and Jeff provided the names of her parents and the address where they lived in London.

Tom called the station and had a patrol car dispatched to the apartments address to escort Mr. Coles to the hospital morgue.

The detectives waited with Jeff till the officer arrived to transport Mr. Coles.

"Damn it." Ed yelled when they were alone again and followed that with a string of curses.

"This psychopath is making fools of all of us and there has to be a way we can stop him."

It appeared even Ed had bought into the criminal profiler's statement that the perpetrator must be a male based on the evidence and pattern.

They headed back to the station to contact the two friends of Jeff Cole and have the forensics technician process Harriet's cell phone.

The telephone conversations with the two friends verified that the fiancée, Jeff Cole had been with them all weekend over eight hundred miles north of London at a hunting camp lodge. They had one vehicle and there was no way that Jeff could have left the camp and come back to London on Friday evening removing him as a potential suspect.

This did not surprise Tom as he was certain that the victim was another random target of the same killer.

The processing of the cell phone revealed the text messages that had occurred Friday evening between the victim and a girl friend.

A call to the girlfriend's number provided the information that Harriet had agreed to grab a late-night drink together as her fiancé had gone hunting for the weekend. She explained that Harriet had been angry at Jeff for going away this close to their wedding date and that he would not be home till Valentines Day on Monday morning.

She stated that the two of them had planned to meet at a local Bar in north London between ten thirty and eleven but she got tied up with a family emergency and texted Harriet that she would have to cancel.

Tom took down the name and address of the bar and thanked her for her help.

Although she was curious about the call the detectives did not elaborate on what had occurred just stated they were following up on an investigation.

Tom realized that soon enough everyone would be aware of what happened as the press had arrived at the barn gate just moments after the police and had been flashing photos and gathering news footage of the scene and the ambulance attendants exiting the barn with the covered body of Ms. Carter.

The Deputy Chief had contacted the Police Chief and the Mayor. Tom and Ed had been told to be at City hall at one o'clock this afternoon for a press conference being held by the Chief and the Mayor.

They knew they would not have to speak, just stand behind the pair of the city officials and add "police" background to the staging of the press conference.

Ed in particular hated what he referred to as the manikin farce as the Uniformed Chief and Mayor would appear to be backed by the detectives and the uniformed Deputy Chief.

There was nothing more that the two of them could do until the criminal investigation team and coroner sent their reports except for the task of contacting the next of kin.

Tom and Ed proceeded to drive to the home of Margaret and Allen Carter located in the west end of London to break the news of the death of their daughter.

When they arrived at the house of the Carters, they noted that it was a well-kept home on a quiet street. Mrs. Carter answered the door and the detectives introduced themselves and asked if Mr. carter was at home. Mrs. Carter responded that he was in the garage working in his woodworking shop.

They asked if they could speak with both of them and Mrs. Carter invited them into the living room and went to get her husband.

Allen Carter was a big man and came into the living room brushing sawdust off his clothes and hands. The detectives introduced themselves again and Allen carter asked what they could do for the police.

"Are you the parents of Harriet Carter?" Ed asked.

"Yes, Harriet is our daughter, what's this about?"

Tom could see the familiar look of fear and apprehension rising in the faces of the Carters.

"Mr. and Mrs. Crater, we regret to inform you that your daughter has been found deceased this morning."

Mrs. Carter looked on in bewildered before she turned to her husband and broke down crying in disbelief.

"How? What happened?" Mr. Carter stuttered as his face and body sank into the shock.

"We believe that Harriet was murdered over the weekend by the serial killer that has been murdering young women in the London area since the month before Christmas." Ed stated. "We deeply regret your loss."

It was obvious that the Carters were not able to comprehend the news of their daughters' demise.

"Is there any family we can contact to come over and stay with you." Tom queried.

"No. Where is my daughter and when can I see her." Allen Carter cried and started to break down as he held his wife seated on the couch.

Tom's heart broke as he looked at the tragic scene and knew that the couple's lives had just been shattered.

"The coroner's office will be in touch with you today to discuss the autopsy and the arrangements for a funeral home to transport your daughters' body." Ed stated.

The detectives again offered their condolences and left the Carters to deal with their grief.

CHAPTER TWENTY THREE

By one p.m. Tom, Ed and the Deputy Chief were all lined up looking stern and professional behind the Mayor and the Police Chief in the media room at City hall.

The Chief started the press conference by stating that a fourth victim of the Christmas Ornament Serial Killer had been located this morning in an abandoned barn on the outskirts of the city.

He informed the press of the name of the victim and that the family had been notified but asked that the Press provide the family with space to grieve their loss.

He continued stating that the police force are diligently pursuing leads to find and stop this menace and protect the citizens of London but there was no additional information that could be released at this point in the investigation.

The Mayor then took the microphone and proceeded to assure the public that the City and the police were putting every available officer on this investigation and he was confident that the perpetrator would be apprehended shortly.

The press conference was then opened to the press for questions.

"Chief, this is the fourth victim of the serial killer over the past three months and he seems to be able to kill at will without the police being able to stop him. What can you tell the public who are frankly afraid to walk the streets?" The reporter for the local newspaper questioned.

"I can assure you that my best detectives are on this case and are working to ensure that the killer is taken into custody before he can kill again." The Chief responded.

"Detective Morgan, I believe you are the lead detective on the case. What can you tell us about the investigation?"

Ed visibly tightened as he looked at the Deputy Chief but no one came to his aid.

"The force has several avenues that we are pursuing based on clues from the crime scenes but I am not at liberty to disclose or discuss those at this time." Ed stated.

"Seems to me that the Detectives are no closer to finding this madman then they were three months ago based on the fact that he can move around the city at will." The reporter continued.

"I can assure you that is not the case." The Chief responded. "We will provide the public with more detailed information when the time is right."

The Mayor then ended the press conference with the statement. "I want to thank the press for attending this press conference and I will continue to be personally engaged with the police to get a speedy resolve to this case. In the meantime, I would advise the public to be diligent and not go out walking the streets alone at night, particularly young woman. Staying together in groups when going out with friends is the best means to defend yourself against this killer."

The press conference broke up and the reporters left but the Mayor asked for the police representatives to meet him in his office. When they were alone the Mayor's anger overflowed as he yelled at the officers that they had to get off their butts and find this killer.

When the Chief tried to assure the mayor that they were working on the case the mayor simply snarled.

" Working on the case is not good enough. The people of this City deserve better than what I am seeing coming from your police force." And then the Mayor turned to Ed and Tom and proclaimed. "If the two top detectives working on this can't get answers maybe they should be back walking the beat instead of sitting comfortably in the police station on their hands."

It was obvious the anger in Ed was at the breaking point. "Your honour if you think you can do better be my guest." He snarled.

The Chief intervened at this point and told the Deputy Chief and the two detectives to leave the office and go back to the station.

As they walked away, they could hear the sound of shouting coming from the mayor's office between the Chief and the Mayor and they could only guess at what was being said.

Tom spend the balance of the afternoon going through the trickle of calls that had come into the hot line over the past weekend. He contemplated the next several days when the facts about the fourth victim would become public knowledge and the resulting flood of calls that they would be inevitably facing as a result.

When Tom arrived home, Ann had prepared a special meal for Valentines Day to thank Tom for his romantic gestures over the weekend. Her parents had arrived and they all sat down to eat together.

Tom tried to keep his conversation light and stayed away from the day's activities knowing that the news reports would reveal the details when they watched at ten o'clock that evening.

After supper the Grandparents bundled up the boys and headed home for the night.

Ann commented. "You have been kind of quiet all evening. Has something happened?"

"I did not want to spoil the evening but we had a fourth young woman murdered this weekend by the Christmas ornament killer and on top of that we got a full chewing out from the Mayor as he feels we are not doing our job." Tom replied.

"Oh my God," Ann gasped. "I am sorry. Let's just relax this evening and try to let it all go for this one night."

Ann cuddled in beside Tom on the couch and laid her head on his shoulder. At ten p.m. that evening they watched the newscast together and saw Tom standing stoically behind the Chief and the Mayor as they made their statements to the press.

The commentator ended the story by stating that it was the opinion of the station that the London Police needed assistance and were possibly not capable of handling the case. They openly stated the resources of the Ontario Provincial Police should be called in to take over the investigation.

Tom tightened up as he listened but Ann soothed him and told him to let it go since the news was only echoing the fear and panic that was evident in the public. She had faith in Tom and his abilities and that he and Ed would catch the individual responsible.

The next morning the hot line was ringing continuously and the department had added ten additional lines and officers to handle the influx of callers. Several of the callers were calling to vent their frustrations with the police force rather then providing leads and it fell on the receiving officers to handle the anger of the public.

The Criminal Investigation report and the coroner's report arrived shortly after lunch.

The corners report was basically identical to the other deaths with the exception of the fact that the victim had sustained a number of cigarette burns to her back and buttocks which he surmised had likely been inflicted prior to the slash wounds on her front side. Her ultimate death had been due to suffocation from the plastic bag being placed over her head to cover her nose and mouth.

The criminal investigation report contained no new evidence that was different from the previous cases, no body fluids or blood except the victims. No fingerprints. They had collected new tire tracks from inside the barn but they could not verify if they were from the time of the crime and the tire prints did not match those taken at the last crime scene for the 1984 Dodge Caravan.

In conclusion the department had nothing new to go on then what they had previously.

Professor Collins was asked to come in and he reviewed the reports to see if there was any update he could provide to the criminal profile.

He concluded that the cigarette burns must represent some other occurrence that happened in the killers past that triggered the addition of that element to the torture.

In reviewing the email, he stated that the killer was becoming bolder in his comments and his obvious dislike for Ed Morgan. The discussion of the red hair for Valentine Day and the fact that he would not be able to find a victim with green hair indicated that the killer was telling the detective when he would strike again.

The next holiday that was coming that tied to the green hair comment was St Patrick's Day in March and that was most likely when he would strike again.

Professor Collins believed strongly that the killer was a psychopath that was not choosing his dates at random but was setting them on a pattern that involved Christmas, New Years, Valentines Day and the next one would be the Friday evening before St Patrick's day.

If this proved true it allowed the detectives a month to try and find the means to stop him if they could come up with some tangible leads.

Frustration was running high in both the department and the City.

Tom and Ed drove that afternoon to the Bar where Harriet Carter had gone on the Friday evening for her last drink.

When they entered the bartender remembered her. It had been a relatively slow night and she had come in around ten thirty and ordered a glass of wine. He recalled that she received a text message close to eleven and had ordered a second glass of wine and spent the next twenty minutes venting about her fiancé and how he had gone away with his buddies hunting for the weekend when they had so much planning left to do for their wedding.

She had concluded her comments stating that it was one hell of a way for her fiancé to show how much he loved her for Valentines day and then she had left before eleven thirty.

He stated that she was not drunk and seemed fine when she left.

He asked her if she wanted him to call her a cab but she stated that she would simply catch the bus at the corner of the street.

"Did anyone pay any attention to her or leave around the same time?" Ed asked.

"No, as I said it was pretty quiet Friday night with just the usual's here and no one left around the same time."

Tom and Ed decided to walk the two sides of the street between the bar and corner bus stop. On the curb about two blocks up from the Bar Tom noticed a gauze cloth on the ground in the gutter and when he picked it up he saw a small spray tube lying underneath it.

He bagged it to take to the criminal investigation team and proceed up the street.

Neither he nor Ed found any other signs of what could have happened on the street.

They went back to the station and Tom gave the spray tube and cloth to forensics for processing.

The next morning the criminal investigation technician advised Tom that the Gauze cloth was the same as the ones found at the three previous crime scenes and contained remnants of the same anesthetic substance. The spray tube contained pepper spray and had been used recently.

It was likely that Harriet Carter had been armed with the pepper spray and possibly been able to use it before she was subdued which would account for the gauze rag etc. being discarded on the street instead of at the crime scene.

The criminal investigation team found only Harriet's saliva on the gauze rag and only her fingerprints on the pepper spray.

The detectives dispatched uniformed officers to canvass the homes and buildings on the street to determine if any residents observed anything on the Friday evening that may help the police. The result of the canvas of the homes found a resident who had seen an unfamiliar car parked on the street just up from their home but the fact that the streetlight was not working had left the resident unable to provide a description. They had noted that a police cruiser had come down the street at the same time and that is what had caught their attention.

Tom contacted the duty desk to find out which officers were on patrol in that area of the city.

They were advised that Officers Kelly and Johnson had been on duty at the time and Tom requested that the dispatch contact the officers and have them stop into the station and see him or Ed Morgan in the detective's department.

Approximately one hour later the officers arrived and Ed asked them if they had been patrolling the street where the bar was located between ten and eleven thirty the previous Friday evening.

Officer Johnson checked his notes and stated that they would have driven through that area on routine patrol between ten thirty and eleven that evening based on their route.

Tom asked if they had noticed anyone in the vicinity or any suspicious vehicles.

Officer Kelley stated that they had not observed anyone but they had noticed a vehicle parked on the street when they drove past and they had slowed to observe the vehicle since it was parked in a darkened area of the street due to a malfunctioning streetlight.

There were no occupants visible. The vehicle was a Ford Bronco according to Officer Kelley's notes that he had made as they passed the car, they noted it was not a 1984 Dodge Caravan that the patrol officers had been advised to be on the look out for.

Tom and Ed thanked the officers and the uniformed patrol proceeded to exit the detective's offices and return to the uniformed patrol section of the station.

"The perpetrator could have switched vehicles after the publicity on the Caravan." Tom mused.

"That's possible, but there is no way for us to verify anything definite regarding the Bronco." Ed replied. "But just by chance lets have the criminal Investigation Technicians run the tire prints from the barn against the Bronco make of vehicles."

Tom contacted the criminal investigation department and asked them to compare the tire marks to those installed on the Ford Bronco.

It was almost time to quit for the night when Tom received the CID report on the tire treads.

The report stated that the tire treads did match those that are used on the Ford Bronco but was also a standard tire that could be matched to a series of other makes and models so they could not conclude that the tire marks were from a Ford Bronco.

Tom went home having come up with another dead-end potential lead.

CHAPTER TWENTY FOUR

The weeks wore on as the detectives checked leads that came into the hot line which inevitably went no where.

Fridays were especially nerve wracking as the police department stepped up the street patrols in the areas of the bars and drinking establishments through out the city. Everyone was on edge looking for the 1984 Dodge Caravan and advised to be on the lookout for any suspicious activity involving a dodge Bronco just to be on top of the situation.

Monday mornings were filled with tension as the task force would gather in the war room and wait while the forensics technician would review Ed Morgan's email account in anticipation of the potential that another email from the perpetrator would be delivered.

The Criminal profiler Professor Collins was confident that the next attempt for the serial killer to abduct another victim was the Friday night before or after St Patrick's day based on the pattern and consistency of the perpetrator's actions.

Professor Collins surmised that the serial killer had demonstrated a high level of comprehension and he was highly intelligent. In addition, he was following a self determined pattern regarding his actions and wanted to ensure that Ed Morgan was aware of his plans. This professor Collins concluded, would allow the perpetrator to feel a sense of superiority and control.

The press continued to run stories daily on the "progress" of the investigation or in most cases stating the lack of progress. They continued to publish stories about the murders and try to find a new spin on the stories that had already been published. Professor Colin had been interviewed extensively and even though he kept re iterating the fact that the criminal profile was only a supporting assessment for the police investigation the press kept stating that 'even though the police had been provided with a description of the serial killer they had still not been able to make any arrests'.

The press had then abandoned Professor Collins and were now quoting all sorts of 'experts' on serial killers to provide their assessment of the case and the handling by police. Most were highly critical of the department and as time passed the news media was grasping for ways to keep their story relevant.

The local city bar owner's association had come together to try and re engage their patrons by making the bars neighbourhoods safer.

The Bar owners had hired additional security staff who would be stationed outside the doors to the bar all evening to keep a vigilant surveillance of the streets around the bar.

When patrons were leaving, they ensured that they were in groups or if a single woman exited the building, they would walk her to her vehicle or call a taxi for the patron.

No women were being allowed to walk the streets alone away from the Bar.

The press had also picked up on the actions of the bar owners association and were heralding them as the ones who were making the streets of London safe for people to go out and maintain a normal routine. The headlines were boldly stating "Bar Owners are taking back the night for their patrons."

The Mayor and the Chief were publicly praising the actions of the bar owners until the psychopath could be caught which they continuously assured the public was imminent.

No one seemed to be hitting on the fact that the press and attention may drive the perpetrator to change his mode of operation and possibly abduct women from alternate locations rather then from bars as he had done so far.

The week of March seventh arrived.

Tom, and Ed discussed the fact that St Patrick's day fell on March seventeenth which was the Thursday between Friday March eleventh and Friday

March eighteenth. They wondered if the perpetrator would attempt to have his next murder on the Friday before or the Friday after the date of St Patrick's Day.

Tom contacted Professor Collins for his input but he could not make any educated assumption on which weekend the killer would use as there was no definitive pattern regarding the actual dates of Christmas and New Year that the killer used in regard to the first three victim abductions.

It would be a wait and see since they still had no definite clues or leads to identify the killer.

After the first week of March the news media had ramped up the fact that the 'clues' received by the police indicated that the Christmas Ornament Killer would strike again around the St Patrick's day holiday and was running a series of statements from all sorts of professional commentators and self titled experts.

It was obvious that the whole city was on edge and the clubs and bars were reporting a noticeable drop in patrons, particularly women.

On the Thursday, Friday and Saturday of March tenth, eleventh, and twelfth the City police force had all available uniformed officers on duty patrolling the streets looking for anything that could be perceived as suspicious. The bar owners had hired additional security staff to be located both inside and outside the establishments.

Monday morning the task force waited expectantly to see if there was an email from the killer to Ed Morgan and the level of overall apprehension was tangible in the police station. The Deputy Chief had joined the waiting group in the war room as the technician scanned Ed Morgan's emails.

By ten a.m. there had been no email and the tension in the room seemed to slowly evaporate.

"Based on his history it appears that we have made it through this weekend but that means we will have to be even more diligent this week. In addition, we want to ramp up our vigilance starting Wednesday night before this Thursday's St Patrick's day. We have no real idea if this psycho will change his pattern." the Deputy Chief proclaimed.

Tom heard what the Deputy Chief had said and was aware that later that afternoon the Mayor and the Chief would be holding a press conference to confirm the fact that the police had not received any emails from the perpetrator or had any reports of missing persons from the past weekend. They would be strongly advising the public to keep on alert through out the week especially on Wednesday, Thursday and Friday evenings in conjunction with St Patrick's day.

Tom had discussed the possibility of the killer changing his pattern to a weeknight two week ago with Professor Collins who had felt that the change would be extremely unlikely.

In Professor Collins observations he felt certain of the base patterns of the perpetrators profile.

"This individual is obsessed with a pattern and in all probability is working full time during the week at an occupation that has interacted with the detectives based on his familiarity and contempt for Detective Ed Morgan.

He abducted on Friday evening and kills his victim over the course of the night, spends Saturday and Sunday in the psychological stimulus of the kill and waits till Monday morning to send his directed email to Detective Morgan to ensure that the body is located on the Monday.

This indicates someone who has the weekend to be alone without fear of making an error and provides him time to gather himself before the police are engaged. This would also indicate that he is in an official position to be able to either observe or receive the information as the police locate the body and the crime scene.

He will be receiving a level of superiority and satisfaction not just from the ritualistic murder itself but from the reactions of the police upon finding the victim in particular Detective Morgan.

This connection to Detective Morgan may be the best lead you have in order to try and identify the perpetrator."

Tom had spent the past two weeks trying to clear his perceptions and to look at any and all individuals who could be engaged with the crime scene and Ed Morgan. He had undertaken discreet background checks on the coroner, the members of the criminal investigation team, the forensics technicians, the dispatcher on the desk, various uniformed officers who were off for the weekend but on duty on the Monday of the dates in question.

He also tried to determine if there were news reporters who could have a grudge against Ed for some slight in the past.

All these efforts turned up nothing concrete that could provide any direction towards narrowing down potential suspects.

He felt that he had to be missing something but everything was far to vague and random to provide any conclusions.

On the Monday evening he sat in his living room and listened to the six o'clock newscast which aired the press conference with the Mayor and the Chief of Police advising the public that the weekend had apparently been free from the Christmas Ornament Killer. The Chief stated that this fact may indicate that the murderer had gone into hiding because of the massive police presence on the streets of the city. The mayor still advised everyone to be diligent over the St Patrick's day week and that the city would keep up its heightened alert. He went on to praise the diligence of the bar owner's association and the individual bar owners for their efforts to ensure their establishments were safe for their patrons. The Mayor concluded by making the statement that the citizens of London would not be deterred from living their lives in a normal fashion by a psychopath that wanted to fill the public with fear. We need to stand up and not let this one individual take away the character that makes this city what it is.

Toms only reaction was to shake his head and wonder how the politicians could be so out of touch with the situation's reality.

Peter also was sitting in his living room listening to the Mayor and Police Chief pontificate on the weekend and on him. He laughed to himself as he considered how wrong they were in their estimations and what they thought they knew.

Of course, there was no body this past weekend as St Patrick's Day was this Thursday which made this Friday the date that he would act.

In addition, the notion that he would seek out other women to punish in the place of his mother on a weeknight was preposterous. He would not force the timeline for the nights activity and the weekend that followed. He cherished his time of solitude and reflection before the Monday morning when he would be able to notify Ed Morgan. A critical component of the weekend was the call out on Monday morning with the ambulance to collect the body and the chance to observe the face of the great detective at the crime scene.

Finally, the city was always on edge for this Wednesday and Thursday with the normal activity that occurred on ST Patrick's Day. The drinking, partying, fights and inevitable injuries required the ambulance service to keep the staff on additional hours and Peter would be working into the night on Wednesday to collect and treat the party goers.

On the Thursday the ambulance services would be attending the St Patrick's Day parade to provide standby medical aid to the revellers.

The week would be a busy one so Peter had already made his choice of bar and a deserted location for the Friday night activities over the past two weeks. He had discretely observed the bar patrons' patterns and had ensured that the site of the weekend activity was abandoned and unused.

The police had devoted all the resources they could for the week starting on the Wednesday evening through the Saturday evening to try and prevent the killer from acting. The addition of the St Patrick's Parade for crowd control had further taxed their abilities and the force was becoming exhausted from the extra hours that were being used by thier limited manpower.

The Ontario Provincial Police were scheduled to provide some back up officers to support the efforts of the city police.

Wednesday evening was plagued by drunken brawls that broke out at bars and private clubs which required the police to respond. Numerous individuals were being transported to medical treatment and the medical services were being flooded.

Tom simply could not grasp the logic that seized people at St Patrick's day to turn the celebration into a drinking binge especially for the university students from the local educational establishments like Western University.

The students held street parties which were attended by masses of young people, drinking and yelling and doing dangerous acts. As the night progressed and the drinking got heavier students would be grasped with a sense of invincibility jumping off roof tops and getting into altercations.

Most young women were seen walking around the streets in groups with friends but others were observed alone which boggled Tom's mind at the stupidity involved. The only thing that Tom could hold onto was Professors Collins assessment that the killer would not break pattern and take what would be an essay victim during this wild night.

Peter was totally engaged in the response and treatment of the party goers. The pain and suffering he witnessed this night were a sight that he enjoyed and eased the demons in his mind for the evening. There had been over one hundred ambulance response calls and all the available units were being utilized. One response call that Peter attended was a fatality where a young man had drunken himself into a stupor that resulted in him stopping breathing. His 'friends' had been so engaged in the street party that they had not noticed him propped up in a corner on the street for several minutes. By the time the ambulance could reach the youth through the crowds the young man had been unconscious and not breathing for an estimate of over fifteen minutes. None of the students either knew how to perform Cardiopulmonary resuscitation (CPR) or were to intoxicated to respond. The ambulance attendances provided first response aid with oxygen but it was apparent the young man was gone and Peter had declared him with no vital signs before they transported him to the hospital where medical staff would declare him deceased on arrival.

Peter had been on shift for nearly sixteen hours when his attendant crew was taken off duty with the knowledge that they needed to be back by nine thirty the next morning to be on standby during the parade. The Thursday shift was to be shortened to allow the team to catch up on their rest before the normal Friday workday.

On Friday morning the street crews were called in to clear up the piles of trash and empty alcohol bottles left strewed about the side streets where the street parties had raged. News reporters aired stories Thursday night of the destruction and the mass chaos of the night before, calling on the University as they did every year to control the students and put a stop to the festivities.

Students would be interviewed claiming that the nights activities were just a way of letting off tension and did not cause any real harm even when confronted by the reporters about the number of injured and deaths. The logic was those hurt or died were just a small number of idiots in the opinion of the other students.

Homeowners affected by the street parties would be on the news complaining about the damage to their properties and the lack of police response to stop this from happening.

All in all, it turned out to be a normal St Patrick's Day for Tom without the discovery of a victim of the Christmas Ornament Killer.

Friday March 18th began with an all-out meeting of the task force in the war room attended not only by the Deputy Chief but the Chief as well.

"We need every officer out there on the streets this evening. No matter what it takes we can not let the serial killer have the opportunity to act again. The public is counting on us. The OPP has agreed to provide additional patrol units to assist in patrolling the designated streets where bars and clubs are located. Any questions?" The Chief stated.

CHAPTER TWENTY FIVE

Peter completed his Friday shift and drove home to the farm where he proceeded to do the normal routine of packing his kit for the evening with the screw hooks, pipe wrench, cord, plastic drop sheet, mistletoe, plastic bags, scuba suit and adult diaper. He packed the scalpel, duct tape, gauze cloth and bottle of anesthetic on top for easy access and completed his preparations with carefully placing the plastic Christmas tree ornament in the glove compartment for safety.

The box that he left on the kitchen table contained only the one remaining ornament and Peter stood quietly considering the fact that after his final activity on Good Friday he would also leave this earth at the completion of his task.

At nine thirty Peter dressed in his long coat and ensured he had his rubber gloves in the pocket and proceeded to drive to the bar where he had chosen to locate his next prey.

Bridgette Summers was twenty-six with blonde hair and a friendly disposition. She was married to her husband Ron Summers who was working the evening shift on this particular Friday evening at the local machinery parts factory. Her sister Ellen and her husband Paul Jones had decided to go to the local bar for a drink and invited Bridgett to come with them.

Bridgett and Ron had talked about it earlier in the day and Ron had told her to go ahead and go, have a nice evening out with her family and Ron would meet her at the bar when he got off work at eleven.

Bridgett, Ellen and Paul went out for dinner at a local restaurant and then proceeded to the bar which was ten blocks from Bridget's home. It was a pleasant evening of laughter and stories about the family. At ten p.m. Ellen and Paul stated that they needed to go home and let the teenage babysitter leave that was watching their young daughter. Paul offered Bridget a ride home but she told them she was fine as Ron had arranged to meet her at the bar at eleven when he was off work.

Hugs were shared all around and Ellen and Paul left the bar.

At ten forty-five Bridget was paged by the bartender to answer a phone call from her husband Ron. There was a rush order that needed to be ready for shipping first thing in the morning and the Manager had required the team working on the line to stay an extra couple of hours of overtime to get the work out. He would not be home till sometime after one. Bridget told him that was no problem and she would see him at home.

Ron told Bridget to call Paul for a ride home or to take a taxi. Bridgett figured that it was late and she didn't want to bother Paul and she decided to not wait for a taxi. She headed out to take the ten block walk to her home. The night was clear and the weather had turned nice from a warm front that had come in during the week filling the air with the feel of spring.

Peter had parked his Bronco on a side street just two blocks from the neighbourhood bar in the town of Woodstock. The smaller town was located a short forty-minute drive from London and consisted of residential and small industrial facilities. It was a quiet town where people knew their neighbours and had not been engulfed in the paranoid panic of London.

It amazed Peter that the distance of a few miles made people feel safe and isolated from the communities they were relatively close too. There were no security guards stationed outside the bar and no regular routine police patrols passing down the street.

He stood in the shadows of a small apartment building alcove and waited until he observed a young woman walking casually up the street towards him. She seemed unconcerned that she was out on the streets, alone at night.

As she passed his location Peter crouched down into the shadows to ensure he was not seen until she was past him and then he silently came out from the shadows and grabbed her around her throat pressing the liquid covered cloth against her mouth and nose. She did not have time to scream or fight back before her mind succumbed to the anesthetic and she fell limp into his arms.

Peter carried her to the Bronco and proceeded to duct tape her mouth, wrists and ankles before he placed her in the back and covered her with a blanket.

Peter slowly drove out of Woodstock heading towards the spot he had chosen in the east end of London for his night's activity.

Ron arrived home at one fifteen in the morning from working overtime and entered the dark house he called home. He assumed that Bridget must have gone to bed and proceeded to make a sandwich in the kitchen.

After eating he quietly went upstairs to the bedroom to undress and go to bed trying not to disturb his wife.

When he entered the bedroom, he noticed that the bed looked empty in the moonlight from the window and decided to turn on the light.

The bed was empty and still made so he walked around the house looking for Bridget.

He was puzzled that she was not there and he decided to call her sisters place even though he knew it was late.

Paul answered sleepily and told Ron that they had left her at the bar at ten when they went home. She had told them she was waiting for him.

Ron explained that he had called her because of having to work overtime.

Paul asked if he wanted him to come over but Ron said not to bother, he would try to contact her.

Ron left the house and drove around the blocks between his home and the bar looking to see if she may have fallen or been hurt but had no luck. He then called the local police station to report his wife missing and to see if there had been any accidents or injuries reported.

The Woodstock police advised him there had been no occurrences over the evening and advised Ron to wait till morning and see if she had gone to a friend or family members for the night. They advised him that they could not consider Bridget to be a missing person for at least forty-eight hours.

Ron spent the balance of the night awake and worried for two reasons. He was worried about his wife's safety and he was also considering the possibility that his wife may have left the bar with another man. Their marriage had been rocky in spots and lately they had been arguing about the fact that Bridget wanted a child and could not get pregnant due to a medical issue with Ron.

He feared that maybe she had decided to turn to someone else.

Bridget awoke from her drug induced sleep feeling the confusion in her mind as she looked around the darkened room. She realized that she was lying on the floor and her wrists and ankles were restrained so that she could not move. She tried to speak but her mouth was restricted by something that sealed her lips and then the realization hit her that she was lying on a plastic sheet completely naked.

Her mind raced to the news articles she had read from London regarding the Christmas ornament Killer as she grasped the fear and shock that assaulted her mind. Her whole being was filled with the terror and helplessness that came with the comprehension of her situation.

"Glad your awake," a voice spoke softly in the darkness from the corner of the room.

A man stood up and moved into the light from the small lantern that was placed on the floor above Bridget's head.

"Hope you like the decorations mother." He continued. "The Mistletoe is just for you the way you did for me, remember."

Bridget was overcome with panic as she lay exposed and helpless on the floor of the room.

"Please God" she prayed in her mind," help me. Somebody please help me"

She felt the sharp sting of a knife blade cut into her legs followed by the same pain in her arms and chest. The pain increased as the knife continued to inflict wounds upon her body until the terror and pain became to much for her to handle and she sank into unconsciousness.

When she awoke her body felt like it was ablaze with pain and she moaned softly with the realization that her mouth was no longer covered. She felt the plastic bag that was over her head before she opened her eyes and looked up through the plastic into the face of the man who was torturing her.

"Don't worry the pain will not last for much longer now mother." He stated as he wrapped a piece of duct tape securely around her throat and she gasped for air against the unforgiving plastic of the bag secured over her mouth and nose.

Ron was still awake and worried on Saturday morning as Bridget had not called or returned. He went out again and circled the streets around their home and the bar.

Paul had come over and joined him as apprehension had risen in Ellen regarding her sister.

Paul kept stating that Bridget was fine when they left and Ron commented that she had told him she would be home when he got off work.

After the bar opened in the afternoon they went to the bar and asked the bartender if he remembered Bridget.

Sure, he responded, she was the lady who got a phone call just before eleven last night and had left shortly thereafter.

Ron asked him if she had left alone and the bartender confirmed that she had.

The panic started to set into both Paul and Ron and they drove to the police station to report what had happened.

The desk officer had them meet with the Sargent on duty and they expressed their concerns.

The duty sergeant assured them that she had in all likelihood gone to visit a friend for the night but he secretly concluded that the young lady was probably off with another man and would turn up eventually.

Come back Monday if she has not contacted you and we will proceed with a missing person investigation in accordance with the guidelines.

I would advise you to stop worrying since they always turn up in a couple of days.

Ron was furious at the police response but realized there was nothing he could do so him and Paul spent the next two days contacting friends and family to see if anyone had seen or heard from Bridget.

Peter had returned home in the early hours of Saturday morning and proceeded to follow his normal routine of washing out his scuba suit and burning the soiled adult diaper. He replenished the supplies in his kit in anticipation of his final activity on Good Friday and stored the kit in the back of his Dodge Caravan to wait for his next and last adventure. He felt it was fitting that Good Friday this year fell on April first, April fool's day and he anticipated the preparations he would make over the next two weeks until that time.

Preparations to end his existence as well since he was firmly convinced that since he was turning sixty this Friday it was the appropriate time for him to be recognized for his actions and he had no intention of going to jail or facing the courts with all their circus like procedures.

He also wanted to ensure that the great detective Ed Morgan would live with the understanding that he could not identify Peter or stop him before he had completed his plan.

He considered again how he had spoken to Ed Morgan all those months ago at the one crime scene and how the detective had not responded, only looked at him with the same contempt that Peter had seen on the face and in the eyes of his dead mother. He wished he could have done more to Detective Morgan but at least the satisfaction of the realization that he had failed in his duty would wipe that look off the detective's face. Peter would ensure that the detective understood how Ed Morgan had played a part in what had occurred and how inept the detective really was in the letter that Peter would write and leave for the detective and all the world to see.

On Sunday afternoon Peter sat and prepared the text of his Monday morning email to be sent to Detective Morgan's email account.

Chapter Twenty Six

Monday morning Tom woke up early from the apprehension and stress that he was feeling. He was afraid that today would be another day of visiting a crime scene at the hands of the Christmas Ornament Killer. He had faith in the actions of the police patrol officers but could not shake the feeling that the killer would find a way.

After he dressed and got cleaned up, he headed to the station.

The weekend had been a quiet one for Tom and Ann after the madness of the St Patrick's Day activities.

They had taken the boys on Saturday to a friend from church's sons eight-year-old birthday party. The party had been complete with a magician which, even though the magician was not that good, had entertained the young group of seven- and eight-year old's. Kevin had been well behaved sleeping throughout most of the time which was a relief for Ann.

Sunday had passed as usual with church service, meetings of the building committee and lunch at Ann's parents' home.

When Tom arrived at the station, he proceeded directly to his desk in the war room and waited for everyone to gather so the technician could review Eds email account.

As they feared a new email appeared in Ed's account from the Christmas ornament Killer so the technician first did the check to see if he could locate the email internet provider address (IP) but the same as before it proved to be a futile task.

Everyone drew close as the technician opened the email and Ed asked Tom to read it out loud to the gathered task force. The Deputy Chief and the Police Chief had again attended the Monday morning task force war room which demonstrated the departments heightened level of apprehension.

"greetings to the 'great' detective Ed Morgan.

I hope you had a restful St Patrick's Day and I enjoyed the speculation that I would be active last weekend and during the weeknights. It was all foolishness on your parts but it is to be expected from the London police force and especially under the guidance of lead detective Morgan.

In keeping with the green, I have left Detective Morgan another present for St Patrick's Day. This present was delivered from the town of Woodstock and has been left in an abandoned warehouse on Dundas street heading toward the airport just before Clarke Road.

Unfortunately, the present does not have green hair but the green mistletoe will have to suffice.

Good hunting and I look forward to us chatting again on Easter Monday which is only two weeks from today.

Signed the Christmas Ornament Killer."

The task force proceeded to prepare to go to the indicated crime scene and Tom advised the Criminal Investigation team as well as the coroner. Patrol officers located close to the scene were dispatched to the scene to lock down the area and prevent the inevitable press prior to their arrival.

The Chief advised that he would contact the mayor and they would attend the scene shortly. It was determined that once the facts had been determined they would lead the resulting press conference.

Tom also had a member of the task force contact the Woodstock police to see if they had any reports of a young woman who may have gone missing Friday evening.

Ed was very quiet on the drive to the crime scene and Tom could see that the tension and embarrassment that he was feeling was causing a great deal of stress for the detective.

"Any thoughts?" Tom asked.

"Ya, I want to catch this bastard who is making a joke out of my career." Ed snapped.

Tom continued the ride in silence realizing that Ed was in no mood to talk.

When they arrived the criminal investigation team was moving through their routine of checking the surroundings outside the building as well as the entrance for any potential evidence. When they could enter the abandoned warehouse, they found the young woman laid out in the same position as the other four.

She was staked out in the centre of a large storage room. Her clothes were piled neatly on a wooden chair that was situated in the corner. She was naked with her wrist and ankles tied by cord to the four screw hooks that were screwed into the wooden floor. Above her head was suspended the green sprig of mistletoe.

Her arms, legs and chest were slashed with long angry wounds and on her stomach was carved the same Merry Xmas.

Even from where they stood, they could see the Christmas Ornament in the victims' mouth under the plastic bag that covered her face.

They had to wait patiently as the coroner removed the restraints and the plastic bag as well as the Christmas Ornament which he gingerly gave to the criminal investigation team to process.

Once he had completed his examination of the body, he called the ambulance attendants to come in with the blanket and stretcher to remove the body.

Peter stared coldly at Detective Morgan and tried to hide his sense of delight and accomplishment at the look of anger and disgust that was evident on the detective's face. He almost succumbed to the urge to go over and say something but he realized that would only draw attention to himself.

When they placed the stretcher next to the body the coroner had them roll the body away from him so he could observe the back of the victim.

Looking for cigarette burns, peter thought, but that was a special for Valentines Day only.

The attendants loaded the body on the stretcher covered with the white sheet and proceeded to exit the building to the flash of cameras and the Television vans that were located now at the scene.

The criminal investigation team had completed their processing of the scene and had bagged the screw hooks, mistletoe, plastic sheet, cord and the victim's clothes for further processing.

They had covered every inch of the room taking fingerprints and as they left Tom looked around the empty room.

In the corner was the abandoned chair and the only evidence of the crime was the small amount of blood staining that had flowed off the plastic cloth and pooled around the edges where it had been on the wooden floor.

The Chief and Mayor entered the room and demanded that Ed provide information regarding the crime in question.

Ed was curt in his replies telling them that it was identical to every other one of the crime scenes with the exception that the perpetrator had not tortured the victim with the cigarette burns like the last one.

The Mayor eyed Ed with what looked like open contempt and the Chief reminded Detective Morgan that he needed to keep his attitudes to himself and behave in a professional manner.

Tom cut into the conversation and advised the Chief and the Mayor that the Criminal Investigation team had retrieved the women's wallet from her belongings and it appears she is a resident of Woodstock which they would confirm and then contact the next of Kin.

Tom mentioned that they should not release the victims name until after they had confirmed the victim's identity. The departments contact with the Woodstock police had revealed that a woman by the same name had been reported missing on Saturday by her husband.

The detectives were going over to the Woodstock police station when they leave the crime scene to follow up with their police department and the victim's husband.

Well, snapped the Mayor, at least we can tell the press that the heightened diligence of the London City police Force had protected the citizens of London as the victim was abducted in Woodstock.

Tom felt a sense of shock and unbelief that the Mayor was going to take credit for the fact that the murderer had to go outside the city to locate a victim.

Tom and Ed left the scene as the Mayor and Chief confronted the gathering of new reporters to hold their press conference and they proceeded to travel the forty minutes to the Woodstock station.

The Woodstock police had contacted Ron Summers and he along with his brother and sister in law, Ellen and Paul Jones were at the station when Tom and Ed arrived.

Tom introduced himself and Detective Ed Morgan from the London Police Force.

'Can you tell us when the last time was you saw Bridget Summers?" Tom asked.

Paul and Ellen explained the activities of Friday evening and then Ron described his phone call to Bridget and the resulting search that they had undertaken. He described the fact that the bartender had confirmed that Bridget had left alone shortly after the phone conversation that she had with her husband Ron.

"Has something happened to Bridget?" Ron questioned and Tom could see the strain and tension on his face. Bridget's sister Ellen had started to cry softly as the realization was coming over everyone that something terrible had occurred.

"Is she hurt or injured. Is she in the hospital?" Ron continued.

Tom took out the licence that they had retrieved from Bridget's wallet and asked if the women in the picture was Bridget Summers. Ron looked at the licence and shook his head affirmatively.

"Mr. Summers," Ed started, "We regret to inform you that the body of Bridget Summers was found deceased this morning in London."

"That's not possible," Ron blurted, "How, why?"

Tom replied, "it appears that Bridget is a victim of the serial killer that has been murdering young women in the London area. The press has named him the Christmas Ornament Killer. Please accept our condolences."

Ellen Jones broke down falling into her husbands' arms.

"I reported Bridget missing to the police on Saturday morning but they refuse to take action. They did nothing to save my wife." Ron sobbed.

"Unfortunately, Bridget was killed overnight Friday so there would have been nothing that the Woodstock police could have done on Saturday." Tom consoled.

"I want to see my wife." Ron stated as the shock set in and fully engulfed him.

"Her body is at the morgue in University Hospital in London." Tom replied. "The Woodstock police can arrange a ride for you over to the hospital if you like but her body will not be available till after the autopsy to be returned to Woodstock. You can arrange transport through the funeral home that you decide to use."

Paul came over and put his arms around Ron and told him that he would take him over to London and help with the arrangements. Ellen was still engulfed in tears of grief as she sat alone in a chair at the side of the room.

Tom and Ed thanked them for their assistance and again shared their condolences.

After the family had left, they requested that the Woodstock police provide them with a copy of the weekend reports that had been given by Ron Summers for their files.

The duty Sargent prepared copies and they left to drive back to London.

The news reports that evening declared the fact that the Christmas Ornament killer had struck again. The press conference from the scene was broadcast on the six o'clock news and Tom sat in amazement as the Mayor fulfilled his intentions and proclaimed that the diligence of the London City Police had thwarted the killer from claiming a victim in their city. The victim had been abducted in Woodstock and brought back to London to complete the murder.

The Chief outlined the crime scene and the murder confirming that everything was basically identical to the other crimes and the police were convinced it was the work of the same psychopath. The 1984 Dodge Caravan that had been a subject of interest in the crimes had not been located along with the driver and he asked that the public continue to be diligent in their caution and to report anything that may be suspicious to the police hot line.

The news cast ended up again with what Tom referred to as the 'talking heads'. Self proclaimed experts of various occupations that would add their summations and opinions. They pulled out past facts that had been reported in the previous cases, flashing the representative picture of the Dodge Caravan and the antique Plastic Christmas ornaments that had been released previously by the police.

As usual the reporters concluded with statements that the London Police were no closer to identifying the perpetrator leaving the citizens of London unprotected and living in fear.

Tom ate his supper in a quiet mood which Ann recognized and allowed him the space he needed to digest his meal and his thoughts. Even Tom Jr and Kevin seemed to sense the tension and were on their best behaviour throughout the evening.

Chapter Twenty Seven

On Tuesday morning Tom went into the station and was confronted by the growing mountain of calls coming into the hot line. Many were complaints against the police which the officers receiving the calls had separated into one pile while any calls that could contain leads were separated into another.

Tom noted that the complaints pile far exceeded the pile of potential leads.

When the newspapers arrived that morning, Tom took a copy of the London free Press to his desk to read the front-page article on the weekend murder.

The newscast media had the advantage of being able to get the news out quicker than the print media but the print media had the luxury of doing more in-depth reporting and utilizing the printed word to expand on the news stories.

The London Free Press had started in London as a weekly newspaper in January, eighteen forty-nine as the Canadian Free Press. It was renamed in eighteen fifty-two as the London Free Press and became a daily newspaper in eighteen fifty-five.

The daily morning edition enjoyed a wide circulation throughout the city and surrounding communities.

The article was prominently centred on the front page and reiterated most of the facts of last nights news cast. In addition, the London police media department had released the name of the victim which was part of the article including an interview with the husband Ron Summers and other family members.

The family reiterated the tale of the weekend and how they had approached the Woodstock police and received no response or assistance. Tom also prepared himself for the tearful faces and anger of the family members who would undoubtedly be featured on this evening Television news cast as the visual media attempted to catch up to the printed newspaper reporting.

Tom realized that there would likely be a public relations storm in Woodstock between the City officials and Police trying to assure the public that there was nothing they could have done at the time. In addition, the Woodstock police had canvassed the area around the bar for any potential witnesses who may have seen someone in the vicinity between ten thirty and eleven thirty on the Friday night in question with no results.

The photos of a 1984 Dodge Caravan as the vehicle of interest in the case and the Plastic Christmas Ornament was predominantly displayed as part of the story.

Tom spent the morning sifting through the leads pile and assigning uniformed officers to follow up with interviews with those that showed promise but he realized that none were likely to be substantive to the case. They were mostly from people who had a hunch about their neighbour who was acting strangely or were sure that the tradesman who had come to their home and did a sloppy job had to be the killer.

There was even one from an angry spouse who was claiming that her cheating husband had all the traits of the killer and she was sure it was him.

At two in the afternoon one of the receptionists on the hot line approached Tom with a sheet of paper.

"I just took a call from a hardware store owner in St Mary's who claims his father believes he sold a box of the antique Christmas Ornaments to a man back in the fall, early September to be more exact."

The paper contained the name of the store owner, his son and the address.

Something in Tom surged with excitement that this may be a real break in the case so he went into Ed's office and explained what they had.

The two of them left the station to drive the thirty minutes to the small town of St Mary's. It was a quaint and picturesque community with a defined town core of businesses and stores.

They entered the small family run hardware store. Tom introduced himself and Ed to the store owner who identified himself as the son of the current owner.

He stated his dad was in the stock room and he gave a shout for him to come to the front of the store.

An elderly man in his mid sixties appeared and after introductions Tom proceeded to ask if they could provide more information regarding their call to the station hot line.

"Sure," Albert Sr replied. "I saw the article in the London newspaper this morning about the murder and the whole story about the Christmas Ornament Killer. When I looked at the photograph of the ornament, I remembered that I had a package of six of those old plastic ornaments here in the store last fall on a top shelf. A gentleman about five foot six with grey hair bought the box. He was in his late fifties."

"My father and mother are semi retired" Albert Jr added. "They left to spend the winter in Florida in late September and only arrived back two weeks ago so they haven't seen the news articles just the comments we have shared about the killings in London."

"Did you get the buyers name or a receipt for the sale?" Ed asked.

"No it was a cash sale. I only remember him because of the look in his eyes as he brought the box to the counter. It was a sort of haunted look the way his face and especially his eyes appeared."

Albert Jr continued from his dads description, "It struck me the hardest when Dad described him because a similar gentleman came in here a few months ago and mentioned he had bought a package of old Christmas Decorations from my father in the fall and wondered if we had any more.

Unfortunately, I didn't think much about it and told him no. We chatted and he bought some nails etc. that he said he needed to repair his barn and left."

"If we had a police sketch artist work with the two of you do you think you could describe the individual?" asked Tom.

Both replied that they could so Tom called the local Ontario Provincial Police office and asked if they could provide a sketch artist as soon as possible.

Tom explained the reasoning and the OPP stated they would have someone there within the hour.

Tom and Ed settled in to wait with the store owner and his son. Tom noted that the people who stopped into the hardware store were all locals and seemed well known to the owners which Tom hoped would help as they were being asked to remember a stranger who had come into the shop.

The police sketch artist arrived and proceeded to sit at a table with the owners as they offered descriptions of the man. Slowly the face took shape until both men were convinced that it was a good likeness of the gentleman who had been in their store and bought the Plastic Christmas Ornaments.

Ed thanked them again for their assistance and they left to drive back to the city.

"This may be the break we have been looking for." Tom commented.

"Too bad the old guy went south for the winter or we may have been able to stop this madman months ago." Ed snarled.

Ed's mood had not improved over the past two days.

When they arrived back to the station Tom had copies of the suspect sketch made and distributed to the staff so that the uniformed officers could canvas the streets to see if anyone could recognize the suspect.

In addition, they had the police media department issue a statement and provide copies of the sketch with the label of 'a person of interest in the Christmas Ornament Killer case' to the press. The press release requested anyone who may recognize the individual to contact the London police.

Tom went home that evening in the most hopeful frame of mind that he had been in for several months hoping that this would be the lead that would put a stop to the serial killer.

First thing the next morning the news cast headlined with the banner Breaking News and highlighted the picture of the person of interest asking the public to contact police if they knew who the individual was.

The hot line phones lit up like Christmas tree lights with callers reporting their neighbours, friends and some family members as resembling the sketch.

Tom took the morning addition of the London Free press to his desk in order to read the article in detail. As he looked at the sketch, he suddenly had a strong feeling of recognition regarding the image. He struggled to identify the connection in his brain until he suddenly remembered the ambulance attendant who had been at the crime scene.

He remembered talking to the individual as his face became clear in his mind that was overlaid on the sketch.

Tom remembered the Criminal Profile. The perpetrator is someone in a professional capacity that had access to interact with the police and in particular Detective Ed Morgan.

Tom jumped up from his desk and hurried into the office of Detective Ed Morgan.

CHAPTER TWENTY EIGHT

Peter woke up and was proceeding through his normal morning routine preparing to go to work. He turned on the morning news cast while drinking his coffee and stared at the sketch of himself on the screen.

The image made him stop cold as he listened to the announcer state that the sketch was of a person of interest in the Christmas Ornament Murder case and asking if anyone knew who the individual was to contact the London Police.

Peter put his coffee on the counter and sat down to think. His plan was to wait till a week from Friday to finish the last of his work before he took his own life but the reality of the sketch left him with the realization that the final step to his plan would not take place.

In a flash of intense thought Peter realized that it was time for him to leave this earth before he could be apprehended.

He took out the last Christmas Ornament and studied it before he went to his telephone and called the ambulance dispatch service to state he was sick and would not be into work that day.

An idea had formed in his head.

He would write the letter to Detective Ed Morgan and then leave the letter and the ornament as a final present for the detective.

Peter knew that he had to win which meant he could not be caught by the detective.

He took out paper and pen and started to write his farewell detailing his childhood and the why for what he had done and to remind the great Detective

Ed Morgan of his incompetence and arrogance. He would outline how the Detective had played a major role in starting the chain of events hopefully to leave the detective with the knowledge that he was responsible.

Tom and Ed called the Deputy Chief and brought him up to date before they headed over to the ambulance dispatch center. When they arrived, they asked for the attendant who resembles the sketch which the dispatcher commented could be Peter Cassidy.

The detectives asked where he was and the dispatcher informed them that Peter had called in sick this morning.

The detectives got the home address for Peter Cassidy and called the deputy Chief to update. The Task Force was mobilized as back up to meet them at the farmhouse listed on the address. The task force uniformed officers had been instructed to seal off the area and not approach the farmhouse or enter the buildings until the detectives had arrived.

The morning routine in London was pierced with the sounds of police cruisers as they proceeded with lights flashing and sirens in the direction of Allenford.

When they arrived, the officers had taken up positions surrounding the property of Peter Cassidy as Ed viewed the scene. The farmhouse was quiet and no lights were seen through the windows.

Ed directed Tom to take uniformed officers and do a search of the old barn that was located off to the right side of the house.

Tom and the officers moved towards the closed barn door with guns drawn. The barn door was full size and slid open on a track so that it was horizontal to the wall.

As they entered the officers moved carefully through the barn interior checking behind the wooden boxes and inside the stall and hay loft.

Tom returned to Ed and reported that the barn was clear but they had located the 1984 Dodge Caravan inside the barn covered with a tarp. Inside the vehicle there was a duffel bag containing the items that matched the ones used at the homicide scenes.

Ed then proceeded to move to the front door of the home and positioned himself off to the side of the entrance.

"Peter Cassidy. This is the London Police Department. We have the home surrounded. Surrender yourself and come out with your hands up."

The officers waited in anticipation for several minutes but there was no response from the house.

"This is your last chance to surrender peacefully our we will use force." Ed shouted.

When there was still no response Ed directed a uniformed officer to attempt to open the door.

The officer was wearing protective clothes and moved in a crouched position to the door turning the knob to determine if it was locked.

The door opened quietly and the officers moved into the front hall of the old farmhouse.

Quickly and methodically the officers moved through the rooms until one officer shouted to the detectives that they had found a body in the kitchen. Other officers called out that the other rooms were clear after which the detectives moved into the kitchen.

On the kitchen floor laid the naked body of Peter Cassidy unmoving on the floor with his arms and legs positioned in a makeshift spread eagle pose. Next to his right hand there was an empty, uncapped bottle. His torso and legs were covered with long scars which appeared to have been inflicted by a weapon such as a belt or whip many years ago.

Tom contacted the coroner's office to attend the scene and the criminal investigation team that had accompanied the task force began the task of documenting the scene by taking pictures of the body and the kitchen. They were also cataloging the items found in the barn.

Tom had them photograph the letter and the Plastic Christmas Tree Ornament that sat predominantly in the centre of the empty kitchen table before he picked up the letter and started to read it to himself. Ed Morgan was standing staring at the deceased with a look that was both relief and disgust.

"Is that a suicide note?" he barked.

"Sort of from what I've read." Tom replied.

"Well you may as well read it out loud so we all hear it without wasting time reading it individually." Ed stated.

Tom prepared to read the letter out loud from the beginning but he was concerned how Ed would respond as what he had read was a scathing commentary against Detective Ed Morgan.

"The perpetrator has a lot of things to say directed against you." Tom commented as he looked at Ed Morgan.

"I'm a big boy and nothing this psycho says will cause me to lose sleep at night now that he's dead." Ed snarled.

Tom proceeded to read the letter:

To the great and useless Detective Ed Morgan.

Since you are reading this letter it is safe to assume you have found me which is no reflection on your ability or lack there of and was likely the actions of the much smarter young detective that you travel with. I am sure that he is the one who is covering your back since I have observed him as the brighter, more capable and more human part of your detective team.

This was not the way I intended our game to be complete as one of my intentions was to leave you questioning for the rest of your miserable life who I was and the realization that this was to be a case you would never solve.

My final plan was for me to use the last of my Christmas Ornaments on Good Friday evening after which I intended to dispose of all the paraphernalia of my kills and the Dodge Caravan that I loved. I would have driven the car into the irrigation pond at the back of my property and sinking the evidence so you would never find it.

Then I would wait a few weeks and 'accidently' get my Bronco stuck on the tracks of a railway crossing coming to work. The accidental death ruling would remove me from this life and would leave you without the ability to identify me and no clue to who the Christmas Ornament Killer was.

I am sure that the death would go unnoticed as an accident the same as when I killed my mother in this kitchen. The table where you found this letter is the same one that I smashed her drunken head against and left her to die. That was ruled as an accidental death caused by her drunken state when she "fell".

The other option would have been to let you know who I am and how you were one of the main reasons I started down this path. To let the world know how I have outsmarted you and exposed you for the incompetent you are.

It appears that option two is the final outcome.

The pills that I have taken this morning were just a precaution as a back up. Good planning on my part as it turns out.

Enough of my spoiled plans it is time to let the great detective know how he fits into this scenario and how he helped me realize my vision.

Detective Morgan, in all his smugness will not even remember how he discarded me.

I attended a crime scene last summer that the great detective was overseeing. I went up to him and introduced myself and asked a simple question. The great one simply looked at me with contempt and dismissed me without stating a response. He turned his back on me and walked away just like my mother had done all my life growing up.

The fury in me was tangible and at that point I vowed to show the detective to be the incompetent bastard that he is to the world.

Therefore Mr. Morgan you were the reason that I embarked on my plan to reveal to the city how useless you really are hiding behind your so called 'great accomplishments'.

In September I came upon the single box of the six Christmas Ornaments in that hardware store that brought back all my memories and that was the catalyst that formed my plan.

As I stared at those ornaments it brought back in clarity the memory of my mother and that one Christmas Eve.

As a child my mother had delighted in the pleasure it gave her when she could hurt me and that Christmas, when she was drunk and angry, she had taken me out to the barn. There she had tied me to the floor naked in the stall. She had beat me with a leather shaving strap leaving the scars that are on my body and kissed my forehead as she sang a Christmas carol under the mistletoe.

She had then taken a tinsel Christmas ornament and crushed it forcing the pieces into my mouth and made me swallow them,

She then proclaimed that I would now have Christmas inside me for the rest of my life.

In the end she had poured a bucket of scalding water over my gentiles and repeated the statement, Merry Xmas to you as she did it.

When I saw those ornaments that looked exactly like the one my mother had used that Christmas Eve, I understood it was time for me to punish my mother as she had punished me. Those women were merely the symbols of my drunken mother.

Through them I could make my mother feel the pain that she had inflicted on me that Christmas.

Valentines had allowed me to also pay back my Mother for the valentine's day she had come into my bedroom and burned my back with her lighted cigarette. To make her feel the same pain that I had felt.

It is ironic in a way that it ended like this.

The last Christmas Ornament I leave as a gift to Detective Ed Morgan so that he has something to remember me and the deaths of all those women that he is truly responsible for.

Farewell and just hours short of my sixtieth birthday I can finally feel peace.

Peter Cassidy.

Tom ended the letter and looked at his senior partner. Ed Morgan was staring stone faced at the body of Peter Cassidy as it lay on the floor revealing to the world all the wounds and pain that he had suffered as a child in this place that was his home.

The coroner had arrived and examined the body and turned to Detective Morgan.

"Not much to guess on here as it is apparent that he died from a drug overdose. I will have the body removed to the morgue if you are finished."

Ed made no reply so Tom Grant told the coroner it was alright to remove the body.

The ambulance attendants came in to place the deceased on the stretcher for transport and the look of shock and disbelief was evident on their faces as they took away a co worker.

Tom told Ed they could go back to the station as the criminal investigation team would complete the cataloguing and removal of the evidence.

Tom instructed the uniformed officers to set up a police line to cordon off the farm and prevent any reporters or the public from accessing the farm once the story was released.

He then called the Deputy Chief and relayed the information that the Christmas Ornament Killer had been positively identified and had taken his own life.

As they drove back to the station Ed finally snapped out of his state of mind and spoke.

"That bastard deserved to be paraded in front of the city and made to pay for his crimes. This was too easy a way for him to go out. He will now become famous of sorts."

When they arrived back at the station copies of the suicide letter were provided to the Chief and the Mayor along with a written summation of the scene. They had called a press conference for that afternoon and they demanded that Detectives Ed Morgan and Tom Grant be in attendance.

At the press conference, as the media cameras rolled and the microphones blared the confirmation that the Christmas Ornament Killer had been located and had taken his own life was broadcast live over the local new channels.

The Chief released the name of Peter Cassidy as the killer and that the evidence had proven beyond any doubt that he was the serial killer. He stated that the detectives of the London Police force had identified the murderer that morning and when they had closed in on Mr. Cassidy to make the arrest the killer had committed suicide.

The Mayor, who had criticized the police over the past three months, was now praising the work of the detectives involved in catching this mad man and preventing him from taking numerous other lives in the city and surrounding areas.

"Our City is once again safe for the citizens to live normal lives and be free from the fear of this killer."

The Chief introduced Ed and Tom as the lead detectives that had solved the case.

Following the press conference, the floor was opened to the reporters for questions.

"Where was the killer found?" "Has the force determined the reasons for his wave of killings?'

"Will all the facts of the case be released to the public since the perpetrator is dead and their will be no trial?"

The Chief responded with the fact that the killer had lived on a farm outside of Allenford, and the crown attorney would be responsible along with the Police force media department to release whatever details were appropriate after the investigation was completed.

One reporter asked for Detective Morgan to describe the scene where the killer had been located and how he had taken his own life.

Ed responded in a quiet tone that the detectives had no further comments as all the information would be coming from the crown attorney's office.

After the press conference ended Tom and Ed returned to the station to finish the write up of their reports.

At the end of that day Tom went home felling drained and exhausted to his wife and young family.

There was no discussion between Tom and Ann about the days events as Ann understood, being a police officers' wife, that her husband needed to process everything that had happened and she gave him his space to do just that.

Eventually they would talk about his thoughts and feelings.

The Monday of the next week when Tom arrived at the station he was called into the Deputy Chiefs office who praised him for his work on the case and proceeded to inform him that he was no longer a junior Detective in training and as such he would be moved to his own office.

He would no longer be partnered with Ed Morgan as his trainer and would work with other detectives as assigned on various cases.

Tom thanked the Deputy Chief and left to go talk with his mentor Detective Ed Morgan.

"The boss told me that he was moving you to be a full detective on your own and I agreed that it was time." Ed stated. "Its been a pleasure working with you this past year."

"I have learned a lot from you and I will always appreciate your skill and guidance." Tom replied.

"Well its good to know someone still thinks I have some abilities." He replied and Tom realized that Ed was still hurting from the revelations that were contained in the dying letter from Peter Cassidy.

"You can't let what that psychopath said get to you." Tom commented.

"Don't you worry about me Lad, nothing that madman said will stop me or what I do."

The Christmas Ornament killer was front page news for several weeks after the conclusion of the case with numerous interviews of Professor Collins as the press wrote up stories to describe and explain the actions of Peter Cassidy.

Reporters tried to dig into the history and life of the killer and the motives for his actions.

It was claimed by a leading crime story author that he would be writing a book that would lay out all the facts on Peter Cassidy.

The bodies had been buried and the farmhouse near Allenford was put up for sale by the estate. Although there were hordes of "interested buyers" who would tour the home of the Christmas Ornament Killer offers were not forth coming regarding anyone wanting to live in the home. It was rumoured that an individual had offered to buy the farm with the intent of turning it into a sort of murder museum.

Detective Ed Morgan had become more noticeably withdrawn since the Christmas Ornament Killer case even though he continued to solve crimes in the City of London.

Three years later Detective Ed Morgan had begun to talk about his retirement but around the time of the year when the Christmas ornament killer case had been solved Detective Ed Morgan was found sitting at his desk having suffered a sudden and massive heart attack.

Detective Morgan had died as he had lived, a senior detective engaged in the work of protecting the citizens of the City he loved.